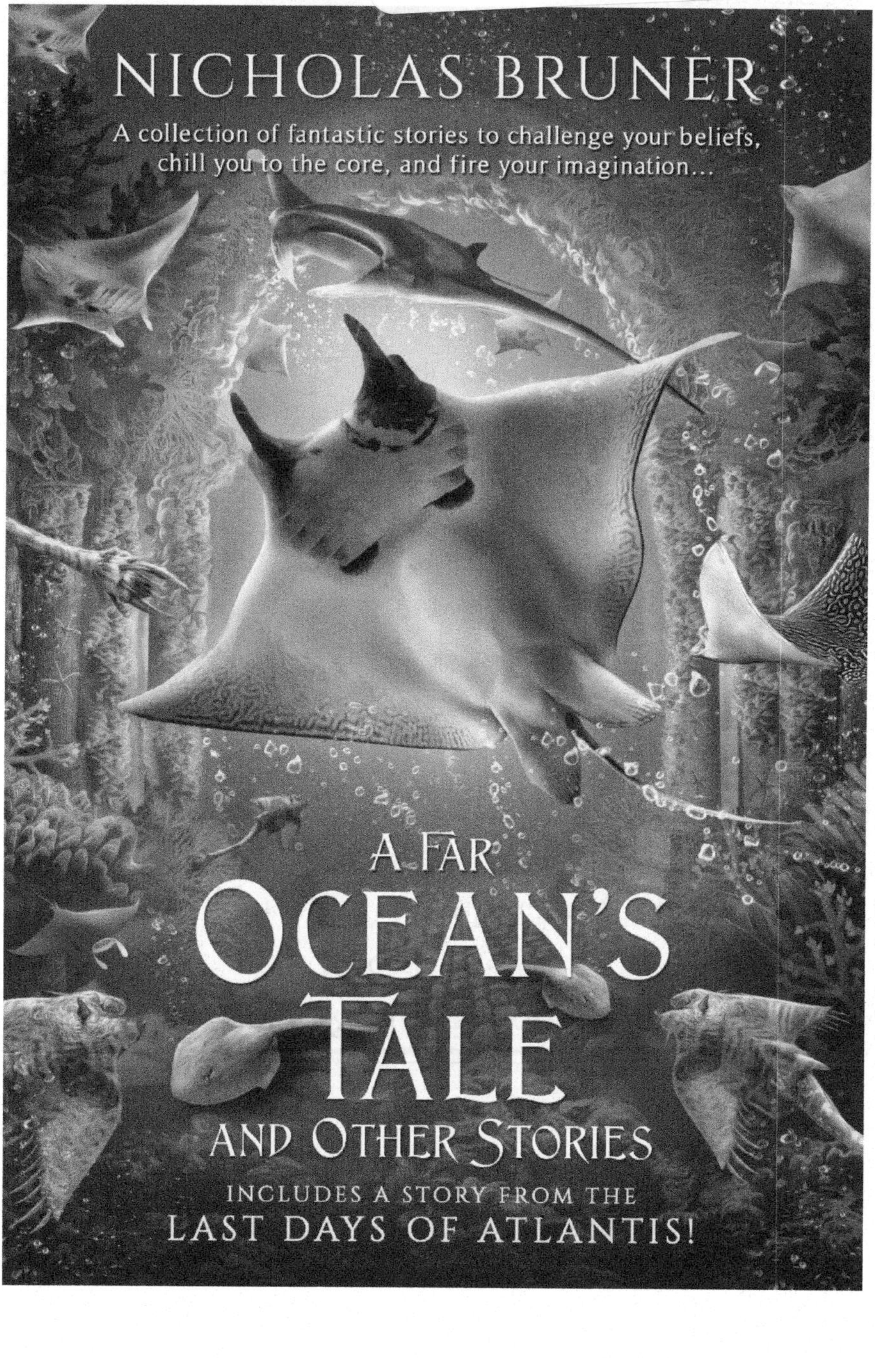
NICHOLAS BRUNER
A collection of fantastic stories to challenge your beliefs, chill you to the core, and fire your imagination...
A FAR
OCEAN'S
TALE
AND OTHER STORIES
INCLUDES A STORY FROM THE
LAST DAYS OF ATLANTIS!

Books by Nicholas Bruner

The Last Days of Atlantis series
Mother Ink (Book 1)
Brother Flute (Book 2)
Daughter Cloud (Book 3)

Other Books
The Ballad of Dani and Eli
A Far Ocean's Tale and Other Stories
Jesus Bugs
The Love Machine
O Trolly Night (Hard Santa Case File Vol. 1) (coming November 2023)
Roll dem Bones

All books available at Amazon (amazon.com/author/nicholasbruner)

Sign up for my mailing list and receive ***Orphan Stone***, the free prequel to the Last Days of Atlantis trilogy!
https://www.subscribepage.com/s8d7d6

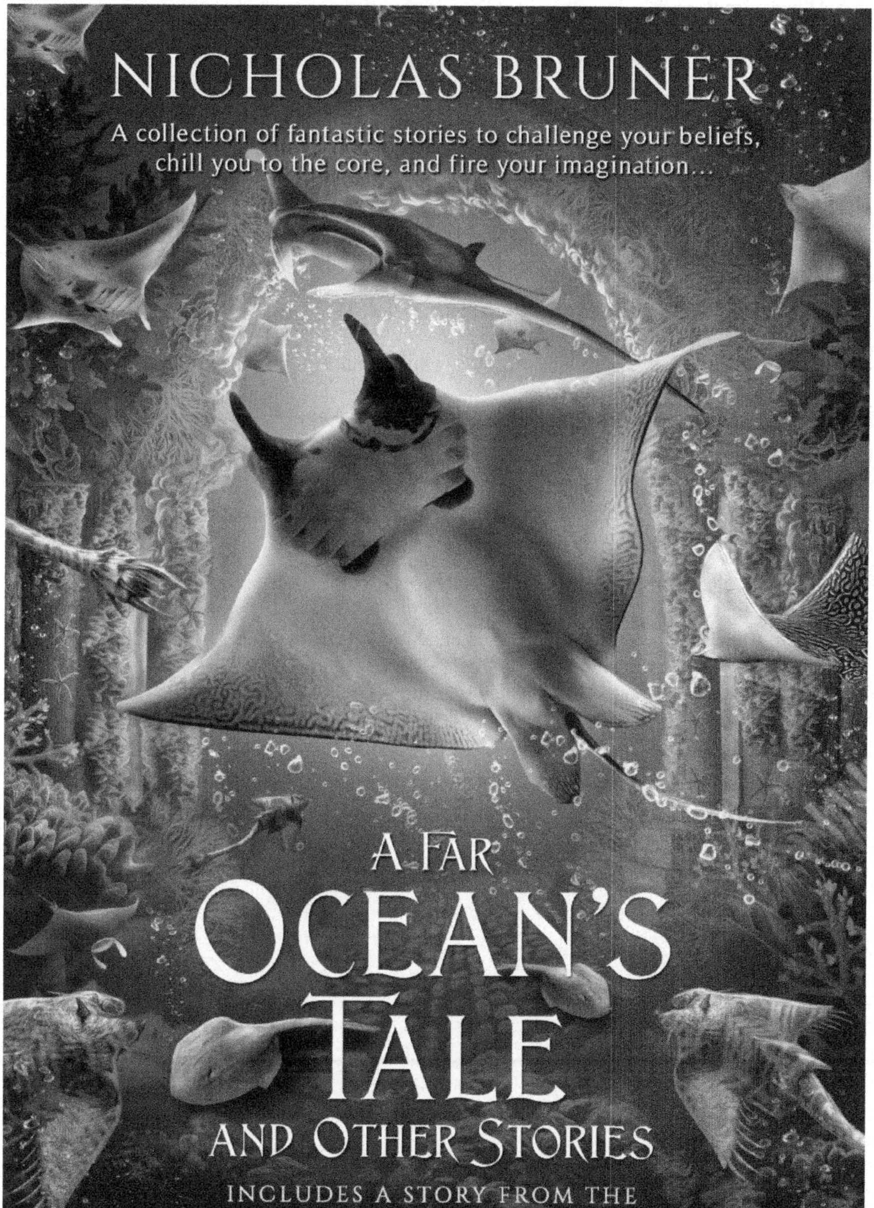
NICHOLAS BRUNER
A collection of fantastic stories to challenge your beliefs, chill you to the core, and fire your imagination...
A FAR
OCEAN'S
TALE
AND OTHER STORIES
INCLUDES A STORY FROM THE
LAST DAYS OF ATLANTIS!

A Far Ocean's Tale and Other Stories

ISBN 978-1-7354892-9-2

Cover design by Moorbooks Design

CONTENTS

DAY OF EMBERS 1

THE TWINS 23

MOUNTAIN MAN 43

LA JOLLA BALLROOM 55

THE METROPOLITAN 77

STEADER 91

FAVOR IN THY SIGHT 107

THE INN OF ROUGH TIMBERS 117

CALIBAN 141

A FAR OCEAN'S TALE 159

DAY OF EMBERS

This story first appeared in the 2022 Writers of Chantilly anthology, Wildlife. *I long swore I'd never write a fantasy story with dragons, elves, dwarves, and other such well-worn fantasy creatures. But my teenage son's favorite fantasy books all have dragons. In fact, dragon books make up the greater part of his reading. I decided to break my vow just once and write this one for him. I hope you enjoy it too!*

The two boys scrambled through the tunnel, the boy in front carrying a candle, the boy in back clutching several small silver coins in his sweaty hand. They came to a bend and halted.

"I think this is it," the boy with the candle whispered. He was smaller and dark-haired and had a shy, bookish air.

"So blow the candle out, dummy," whispered the second boy, taller, fair-haired, and athletic. "He's doesn't like light."

"How will we get back out if the candle's out?" the smaller boy asked.

"Easy, don't you remember the way?" the taller boy replied.

"I guess. Can I have my coins, then?"

The taller boy handed the smaller his share of the groschen, and the smaller boy blew the candle out. They proceeded around the corner, blind in the dark but able to perceive by the changing sounds of their footsteps that they had entered a much larger space. The ground here changed as well, switching from rock to a light clinking, as if they stepped on piles of loose metal.

The two boys halted, not sure if they should go farther, or what else to do. "Is he here?" came the whisper of the smaller boy.

Ten or twelve lachters away, a crescent of glowing crimson appeared in the darkness, and then a second next to it. Eyes. The two boys held their breaths.

"Did you bring something for me?" an impossibly deep voice

growled, not too loud yet seeming to fill the space, resonating within the very walls.

"Y-yes," the smaller boy said, holding out his groschen.

"Just drop them, if you please," the deep voice said.

The smaller boy dropped the copper coins. The taller boy pantomimed dropping the coins with his right hand at the same time, but actually slipped them into his pocket with the left.

"Tell me, who are you to dare disturb my slumber?" the deep voice asked.

"I-I'm Joachim," the smaller boy said. "And this is Gerdt."

"Shut up, you idiot," Gerdt hissed at Joachim. Louder, to the red eyes, he spoke, "O mighty one! We come to behold your magnificence and to bask in your glory."

"Do you now?" Something in the deep voice seemed amused. "Do you really wish to bask in my glory? Or do you wish glory for yourselves, mmm?"

The second boy hesitated a moment, then went on. "We…we hope being in your presence will reflect a bit of your own glory onto our meager—"

"We want to show how brave we are," Joachim broke in. "The older boys said we wouldn't do it. Jens said we wouldn't dare, and then Gerdt said he was as brave as any of them, and he would too do it, and that's when I said I'd go with him."

"Shut. Up." Gerdt spoke through gritted teeth.

"Well, you've proven your bravery," the deep voice said. "Now go, and leave me in peace."

Joachim turned around, but Gerdt stood his ground. "Not yet. We brought you coins. Now you do something for us. That's the deal, isn't it?

The crimson eyes narrowed. "That is indeed the tradition. What is it you would have me do for you?"

"Proof," Gerdt said. "I need proof I really came down here."

"Proof. Very well." Below the crimson crescents, an incandescent maw opened, a flash of teeth, a sound like *pffft.* A glowing orange glob arced through the air toward the boys and landed with a sploosh on Gerdt's cheek. The impact flung glowing strands across his neck and ear and up to his hairline. Skin sizzled and hair singed.

Gerdt screamed in pain, turned, and dashed the way they'd come, tripping and picking himself back up, heedless of the darkness, of his torn trousers, of all but the crackling, bubbling flesh where the saliva had hit.

Joachim ran after him, but it felt as if legs didn't move his body. He pushed with all the strength in his legs but went nowhere. He reached behind him to check if he was caught on something, and felt a hard, scaly toe inserted in his belt. In the dark, he began to panic.

The deep voice spoke, closer now, almost in his ear. "Calm yourself, young one. Slow your breathing." The bass notes of the voice rumbled through his bones.

Joachim tried to obey, forcing himself to inhale deeply and exhale fully, but his heart beat like a galloping horse. "Are you…going…to kill me?" he asked in between breaths.

A deep sound, like a chuckle. "Kill you? Not today. But I didn't want you to leave without your favor."

"I don't need a favor," Joachim said. "I just want to go."

"I suppose I must be in your debt then," the voice said. "Come back again someday when you think of something I can do for you. Perhaps you will have a question my wisdom can answer."

The toe removed itself and Joachim stumbled from the sudden release. He picked himself up and followed his friend as fast as his feet would carry him.

* * *

The young man made his way carefully down the tunnel with the dark lantern. At the bend, he slid the shutter on the dark lantern closed, obscuring the light, and set it on a flat stone near the wall. He slowly walked around the curve and to the threshold of the main chamber, where metal crunched under his feet. From his pocket he withdrew two gold coins and tossed them out. They landed with twin clinks.

Two red crescents appeared and bobbed up and down, the sound of sniffing coming out of the darkness. "I recognize that scent," the deep voice said, and as before the walls shook with sympathetic vibration when he spoke.

"You said last time I could come back if I had a question," the young man said.

"So I did," the voice said. "But I didn't expect it would be so soon."

"It's been five years," the young man said.

"Mmm. So hard to tell down here, so hard to tell." The red crescents blinked. "The name was Joachim, I believe?"

"Your memory is astounding," the young man said.

"Not really," the voice said. "You claim it was five years, but I'm not so sure it wasn't last week. But tell me Joachim, what question do you bring me?"

Joachim hesitated, swallowed. "It's about...well, it's complicated. You see, there's, well—"

"It's about a female, isn't it?"

"Yes," Joachim said. "How did you know?"

Another of those deep, wall-quaking chuckles Joachim remembered from last time. "Never mind that. Tell your problem to me."

"Well, she seems to like me. I mean, we laugh a lot when we're together. I'd like to ask her to marry me, but I don't know if she'll say yes."

"Mmm." The crimson eyes went up and down, as if the head were nodding. "But why wouldn't she say yes?"

"Her father's a butcher, for one thing, and my father's only a farmer. And she's so pretty. It's hard to believe she could ever be pleased with someone like me."

The eyes narrowed a bit. "Have you tried strutting in front of her, showing off the sharpness of your claws and the length of your tail? Roaring so she can see your fierceness? And then snatching her and carrying her back to your lair, snapping your teeth around her neck if she dares to protest?"

"I...I don't think that would work, in this case."

"No?"

Joachim turned to go. "Thank you anyway."

"Wait." Not a suggestion, a command.

Almost involuntarily, Joachim turned back around. When he did, the eyes were right in front of him, mere inches away, and in their faint glow he could see the long, scaled snout, the flared nostrils with a bit of steam puffing out, the lower teeth curving up around the upper jaw.

"Do you love her?" the dragon asked.

"Yes." As scared as he was, Joachim's voice was sure. The dragon's eyes stared into and through him and Joachim felt like a sheet of old, wrinkled vellum, folded and re-folded so many times that light shines through the cracks.

"Mmm," the dragon said. The eyes blinked and withdrew, and there was a clinking and clanking, as if someone were rummaging through a drawer. "Ah, yes, here we are."

Joachim felt a hard, cold claw in his hand, and then something metallic slipped into his grasp. "What is it?"

"A loan," the dragon answered. "But that's not what you meant, is it? Let me explain. It's a golden bell. Given to me once by a duke, who hoped to save his life. He claimed that if you ring it three times in the presence of a woman pure of heart, she'll fall in love with the next man she kisses."

"And he gave you this bell and saved himself?" Joachim asked.

The deep chuckle. "I crunched his bones like kindling."

"Oh." Joachim shivered. "Anyway, thank you so very much. I'll return it as soon as I can."

"No need to hurry," the dragon said. "But do not forget, for it will go badly for you if I must crawl from my home to restore my hoard. Do not make me wait so long as the seventeen hundred and ninety-two days that passed since your last visit. And

Joachim, one more thing."

"Yes?"

"I wish you good fortune with Gisela."

A startled exhalation. "But I never told you her name!"

"You'd be surprised at how well sound carries up the mountain from the village, when the conditions are right." The crimson eyes disappeared, and there came a sound of a huge weight settling on metal. "Fare thee well."

Joachim retreated and retrieved the dark lantern. He was about to slide open the shutter when he hesitated, turned around, stepped back around the corner. He called out, "You know my name, but what can I call you?"

The red crescents blinked open, and blinked again in surprise. A long slow inhalation that caused twin nostrils to glow orange beneath the crescents. "Centuries I've lain here, and in all that time, no human has ever asked me my name."

Joachim waited, but no further answer seemed forthcoming, so he turned and opened the shutter on the dark lantern. As he was about to take a step, the voice intoned, "Ask me again when you return."

"Because you need time to decide whether to tell me?" Joachim asked.

"Because I need time to remember it."

* * *

The groom picked his way down the tunnel, the light from the dark lantern guiding his way. At the bend, he slid the shutter closed and proceeded to the threshold of the great chamber. He took a silver goblet from a bag and cast it out into the darkness, where it landed with a clanging splash.

"Joachim." The deep voice resonated and the crimson eyes opened. "Your offerings become more precious."

"Part of a set of eight, a gift to us from my father-in-law," Joachim said. "It seems a share must surely go to the one who made the wedding possible."

"Ah, so you're pair-bonded, then," the dragon said.

"Yes, if that's how you'd like to put it." Joachim withdrew the golden bell from the sack and rang it once. The sound was pure and cool. "And I haven't forgotten this either. But I'm not sure you want me to throw it."

"Indeed not," the dragon said, and Joachim felt a claw taking it from his hand.

"Tell me something," Joachim said.

"What question do you have?"

"Is the bell really magic? Or did you just give it to me as a way to bolster my confidence to ask Gisela for her hand?"

The crimson eyes flashed and loomed before Joachim, and the dragon's voice roared. "Little man, do not presume to doubt the truth of my words! When I say something is a fact, it is as certain as diamond!"

Joachim stumbled back, catching himself painfully on a stone outcropping with his hands. "I—I—"

"And besides," the dragon went on, his head pulling back and his voice returning to normal. "It worked, didn't it?" A deep rumbling chuckle.

"I'm not sure I fully understand your sense of humor." Joachim pushed himself to his feet and checked his body gingerly for blood or bruising.

"Give it a few hundred years," the dragon said. "It'll come to make sense."

"Well, thank you for the loan of the bell." Joachim turned to go.

"Wait," the dragon said. "You didn't ask for anything."

"I don't have a request this time," Joachim said. "I was just returning what belonged to you."

"Then let me give you some advice," the dragon said. "The friend of yours, who came with you on your first visit. Gerdt, was it?"

"Yes, Gerdt is his name, although I'm not sure I'd call him a friend," Joachim said. "He's never forgiven you for disfiguring his face, you know."

"You mean he's never forgiven *you*," the dragon said. "I'm a force of nature. Can't do anything about that. But you're the little runt who tricked him into coming in the first place."

"That's not how it happened!"

"I don't claim that's how it happened," the dragon said. "I only speak of what's in Gerdt's heart, which has grown so rancid with bitterness that I can smell it from up here. Be careful with him."

"I will," Joachim promised lightly. "Thank you for the warning." He turned and took a few steps up the tunnel.

"Maybe don't leave yet," the dragon said.

"Maybe?" Joachim halted.

"I don't…." Quiet for a moment, and suddenly, more of the clanking of metal on metal that suggested rummaging through a great heap of treasure. "Yes. Yes, I think I have something else in here that might help you." Several minutes of clanking ensued. "Ah, this is what I wanted."

Joachim felt a claw open his hand in the darkness, and the claw inserted two items in his palm. He ran the fingers of his other hand around the items—cool metal, round, with a hole in the center, and a sharp point at one spot, as of a mounted stone. "Rings? Another loan?"

"Not a loan this time, but rings, yes," the dragon said. "More than just rings, though. These belonged to a duchess who ruled when even I was not much more than a hatchling. She had these silver rings mounted with emeralds, for there was treachery afoot in her kingdom, and she feared for her life and the life of her toddler son. She claimed that anybody who tried to do her or her son violence would instantly have his soul entrapped in the emerald until she released him."

"And how does one release a soul from an emerald?"

"I believe she said by tapping it against a certain stone three times."

"Thank you, but I'm not sure I have need of these," Joachim said.

The eyes narrowed. "Is it wise to turn down a gift from a dragon?"

"Er, I see your point," Joachim said. "I'll put this one on right now, and the other will look lovely on Gisela's hand." Here Joachim gave a bow in the dark and turned again, climbing back around the bend.

"Dies-Favilla," the dragon said before Joachim could go.

"I'm sorry?" Joachim said.

"My name," the dragon said. "It's Dies-Favilla. You can remember it for next time. Should you ever return, I mean."

* * *

The new father made his way down the tunnel, less carefully than in the past given his familiarity with the way. He closed the shutter on the dark lantern and turned the bend, carrying a sack in his other hand. At the threshold, he listened for a moment, hearing the regular breathing of the great beast in the darkness, the exhalations loud as a bellows. Was the dragon asleep? Did he really not wake until he heard the clink of precious metal?

From the sack, Joachim took out a pair of candlesticks and lobbed them into the darkness. They landed with twin clunks and two crimson crescents appeared.

"Pewter," Dies-Favilla said. "Not as valuable as last time."

"But these are candlesticks engraved with a pattern of a great wurm breathing fire on the one, and a man in armor with a sword on the other," Joachim said. "When I saw it at the curiosity shop, it seemed appropriate."

"Indeed," Dies-Favilla said. The crimson eyes neared Joachim and the nostrils came so close the rising steam heated his face. The dragon breathed in slowly, as if taking in a scent, then the crimson eyes retreated again into the lair. "You have a young one now. I can smell it."

"Yes, a little girl, six months old," Joachim said.

"What is her name?' Dies-Favilla asked.

"Alexandra."

"Ah, a beautiful appelation."

Joachim smiled. "Thank you. I could bring her for you to—"

"No!" Dies-Favilla said, and there was a touch of panic in those reverberating tones.

Joachim fell back from surprise and the force of the sound. "I-I'm sorry. I didn't mean to offend you, Dies-Favilla."

"Mmm." The crimson crescents widened a bit. "I'm not offended. It's only that young virginal human females…they awaken appetites in me that are best not awakened."

"I see," Joachim said. "And you wouldn't be able to help yourself."

"Perhaps. Perhaps not. Best to avoid the temptation." The crimson eyes narrowed. "What of this antique shop you speak of? There's no such place in the village I'm aware of."

"My father-in-law again." Joachim sighed. "Before Alexandra's birth, he had us travel to Ingoldstadt to buy things for her nursery."

"Ah, Ingoldstadt," Dies-Favilla said. "I knew the duke there once. But you sound as if you didn't enjoy the trip?"

"I simply don't see what good all this luxury will do for the baby. She doesn't care about any of it. It's simply so my father-in-law can keep up appearances with his neighbors around the town square."

"So marrying into Gisela's family has proved a mistake?" the dragon asked.

"I didn't say that," Joachim said. "Not at all. I still love Gisela and Alexandra with all my heart."

"Yes, I believe you do," Dies-Favilla said. "Keep one eye on your mate and your young one. I will be angry if any harm should befall them due to inattentiveness on your part."

"I will," Joachim said. He turned to go.

"You don't have any requests this time?" the dragon asked.

"Not this time," Joachim said.

"Nor did you have any loans to return. So why did you come?"

"Well," Joachim said. "You're up here all alone, going years without seeing anyone."

"Silly villagers come up from time to time to interrupt my napping and ask for advice," Dies-Favilla said.

"How often is that?" Joachim asked.

"Oh, once or twice a year, I suppose."

"It seems like you don't have anyone to talk to, that's all." Joachim hesitated. "I thought perhaps you could use a friend."

A sharp repeated tapping sound came from somewhere in the dark, and Joachim imagined dragon claws drumming against the cave wall.

"Leave me now." The crimson crescents turned away. "Dragons have no need of friends."

* * *

The girl made her way down the tunnel, a candle flickering in one shaking hand and groschen gripped in the sweaty palm of the other. She halted where the tunnel bent, memorizing the arrangement of the stones on the ground. Then she blew out the candle and made her way down, halting when the surface under her feet switched from stone to loose coins.

In the darkness, two red crescents observed her already. She opened the palm of her right hand and flung the groschen as hard as she could. The coins tinkled where they landed.

"Alexandra," a voice intoned, so deep it vibrated through the very walls.

"Y-yes, that's me," the girl said. "How do you know my name?"

"I know many things you would not expect," the voice said. "How old are you now, child?"

"I'm seven years old." Alexandra hesitated, and when no reply came, ventured a further question. “How old are you?”

“Do you know your times tables?”

“Yes. Sort of. I mean, I’m working on that with Mama.”

“Well, I am seven times seven times seven, and thrice that again,” the voice said. “You can ask your mama what that comes out to.”

“Are you really a dragon?” Alexandra asked.

A deep rumble, like chuckling. “I am a dragon through and through. Tell me, Alexandra, how fares your father?”

“He doesn’t fare well,” Alexandra said. “He’s in jail now. That’s why I’m here.”

“Mmm.” The crescents narrowed. “And he sent you to get my help?”

“No,” Alexandra said. “He doesn’t know I’m here. But I know if anyone can help him, you can.”

“Why do you think I have that within my power?” the dragon said.

“I—I’ve watched him come up here sometimes, when he didn’t know I’d followed him. And the older kids say a dragon lives in here, and there are rules to make him help you. I didn’t know if I believed them. Until now, I mean.”

The crimson crescents approached Alexandra, and below them was a snout emitting steam and a mouth with curved teeth. A forked tongue flicked out and ran across the dragon’s lips. When he spoke, the walls shook with the sounds of his words.

“First of all, there are no *rules* to make me do anything. There are traditions, and I choose to follow them as it pleases me. Second, little girl, it was extremely foolish of you to come here today. Don’t you know what dragons do to little girls like you?”

“They…they…” A bit of urine trickled down her leg. “They eat us up?”

“Smart girl. We eat you up. And it is a long, long time since I have fed.”

“But you can’t eat me up!” Alexandra burst into tears. “What about my papa? He’ll be in jail forever, if Herr Fasche doesn’t wake up."

A slow exhalation from those nostrils, and the steam surrounded Alexandra in a cloud so hot and moist it wet her clothes and left sweat dripping down her temples. The crimson crescents retreated back into the darkness.

"So. What of this Herr Fasche? Tell me about him."

The girl took heaving breaths, trying to get ahold of herself. "He—he has a horrible face, covered with scars on one side. Mama said he got burned one time."

"Yes, I believe I know him by a different name," the dragon said. "And what do you mean if he doesn't wake up?"

"He and Papa got into a fight, and Herr Fasche tried to hit Papa, and then he fell to the ground." Her eyes welled up again. "Papa didn't even hit him at all! But everybody said he must have, and that it's his fault Herr Fasche fell in a…I can't remember the word."

"A coma?" the dragon suggested.

"That's it," Alexandra said.

"When did all this happen?" the dragon asked.

"A few days ago, on New Year's Eve. We went to Gaw-paw's house for a party, the big one he has every year with all the people there, and Mama told Papa not to drink so much as usual, and Papa said he had to or he wouldn't be able to bear it at Gaw-paw's, but I don't know why he said that, because it's always fun at Gaw-paw's house."

"I see," the dragon said. "And what do you think the fight was about?"

"Herr Fasche…he said things to Mama, in a room at the top of the stairs. I didn't understand it all, but he called Papa a dreamer, although Papa wasn't even sleeping, and he said Mama deserved better. And I think…I think she agreed with him."

"But how did you hear all this?" the dragon asked.

"I shouldn't say," Alexandra said.

"You won't get in trouble with me, if that's what you fear. But I need to know the whole story if I'm to help."

"Okay." Alexandra swallowed. "Nobody knows it, but I was in the room across the way, where Gaw-paw keeps all his fancy plates and things I'm not supposed to touch. In fact, I'm not supposed to go in there at all, but everyone was busy downstairs so I knew they wouldn't see me go in there. And then I think Herr Fasche tried to touch Mama, and she said, 'How dare you!' just like that, except louder. Then Papa came up the stairs, and that's when it happened."

"Do you visit your Papa in jail?"

"I went with Mama once, but after that she said it's no place for little girls. But she goes every day, and it's not fair that I can't go too."

"Indeed, it's not fair at all. I think tonight when your mother goes to the jail, you must throw a tantrum, and scream and cry and refuse to be consoled until she has no choice but to take you with her."

Alexandra tilted her head and gave the dragon a look. "How did you know Mama goes to visit him at night? I didn't say that."

"Never mind that. When you get there, tell your father that you came to see me, and that I have told you to return with the ring set with an emerald that he wears."

"But I'll get in trouble if I say I came here!"

"You'll have to admit it anyway," the dragon said. "Which is worse? You getting in trouble, or your father in jail?"

Alexandra lowered her head. "Papa in jail."

"So it seems to me your choice is clear."

"Okay, I'll do it." Alexandra set her jaw and turned to go. She patted her hand on the ground, trying to find where she'd set the candle. Unexpectedly, the waxy candle inserted itself in her hand.

"One more thing," the dragon said, and his voice was directly behind her. "If your father doesn't want to give you the ring out of some misguided attempt to protect you, tell him I said that the loan of the ring is over, and my payment if I don't get it back will be to come out from my lair and gobble you down whole. Now hold the candle up."

Alexandra lifted her trembling hand. A tiny puff came from behind her, and the candle lit. She ran shrieking all the way to the entrance.

* * *

The girl crept down the tunnel. She carried her father's dark lantern, and at the bottom she slid the shutter closed and continued the rest of the way in the dark. Again, the crimson eyes waited for her. From a pocket she withdrew a fork and threw it in the air. It landed with a ping.

"Silver," the dragon said.

"From Gaw-paw's special room," Alexandra explained. "He'll never miss it."

"And do you have the ring?" the dragon asked.

Alexandra reached in her pocket again and pulled out a gold ring with an emerald setting. She held out her tiny hand in the dark. She was going to explain about going to the jail with her mama, and how when she told her father about her visit to the dragon, she didn't get in trouble at all. But before she could speak, the crimson eyes loomed, the breathing grew louder. The eyes stared through her, and she felt like a lump of wax before them, melting and unable to keep her corporeal form, as if the dragon might slurp her up. Then cold claws removed the ring from her palm with surprising delicacy.

"Leave. Now." The dragon's voice was deep and loud and urgent.

Alexandra turned and ran down the tunnel, not even stopping to retrieve the dark lantern, though she was sure to catch trouble for losing it, not even crying when she tripped in the dark and scraped the flesh off one elbow. And as she dashed out the cave's entrance onto the stony path trailing to the half-timbered houses of the village at the bottom of the mountain, she heard the rattling of scales behind her, and felt a rush of hot wind, as if the air was being forced out of the tunnel. When she looked up, she saw something that most people will never live to describe: a dragon taking flight, its immense ebon-scaled body seeming to take forever to fully emerge from the cave, segment after segment streaming forth like black water gushing from a burst dam. It ascended into the late evening twilight, ribboned against the vast sweep of stars and moon, headed toward Ingoldstadt in the northeast.

* * *

How many years had it been since Dies-Favilla had ascended into the clean night sky? Many, many, almost longer than he could recall. It was a fine evening, full of stormy clouds crackling with lightning, and he sailed up high in the air, just for the delight of it, higher, higher, as if to reach the moon.

The girl had sparked something inside him he hadn't felt in a long time, a feeling only virginal human females could create, with their flowered aroma, and their exquisite beauty, and that ineffable something that stirred male dragons so much that could best be described as purity, or maybe naïvety. What he wouldn't love to do…. But this one was too young, and besides, her father was a frie—no, that wasn't it. Well, anyway, Joachim was a human that Dies-Favilla had far more respect for than most humans. He was thankful that when he had asked the girl to run, she'd had the sense to obey him, while he'd still been in control of himself.

But now he rose so high the atmosphere grew thin, and Dies-Favilla felt his furnace going out inside. He let himself fall, until the air grew thicker and he could breathe again. It took much effort to resume his flight, to get his bearings. He was out of breath, he was tired. Once, such a flight wouldn't have had such an effect on him. But he was not the same dragon he had been centuries ago. Alexandra may have stirred feelings he had not felt since he was young, but he could not deny his age. He probably didn't have all that many years left, in fact.

Eventually he reoriented himself, located Ingoldstadt on the plain before him. It had grown far larger than the last time he'd seen it, but still, the Duke's castle was there on the hill. And somewhere in it, the magic stone to tap the emerald against. As he rushed over the parapets, he could even catch a whiff of the magic. Yes, it was in there somewhere, though he might have to take the castle apart to find it.

Dies-Favilla grinned. That sounded like an enjoyable task. He wondered if the Duke's descendants still resided there. He hoped so.

* * *

The middle-aged man cautiously stepped down the tunnel, taking his time to assure his footing. At the end, he slid the shutter closed on the lantern and stepped around to the lip of the chamber he knew so well, if by smell and sound, rather than sight.

He rummaged in the pocket of his fine pants for a pocket watch and held it out. "You might want to take this one. It's a bit delicate."

The crimson eyes opened and in the dark he felt the dragon claw approach. He dropped the watch into the scaled talons.

"You know, you don't need to always bring such valuables," Dies-Favilla said. "At this point, the simple coins of our first meeting would be sufficient."

"And yet, if I came empty-handed, I imagine you would spit a burning dollop of dragon saliva across my face," Joachim said.

"I'd do much worse than that," Dies-Favilla said. "For you know better. I was being merciful to your friend Gerdt Fasche. How goes it with him, by the way?"

"Same as ever, I suppose," Joachim said. "He's never spoken to me since he woke up from his long nap."

"It turned out for the best then," the dragon said. "And what about Alexandra? If I'm not mistaken, I believe my ears heard a harp playing wedding music a few weeks ago. But sometimes it's tricky to tell, all the way up here."

"No, you're correct." Joachim smiled in the dark. "She was as beautiful on her wedding day as Gisela was on hers. And her young man is a far sight more promising than I ever was. He certainly required no bell to make her fall in love with him. And of course, her grandfather insisted on spoiling them with an excess of wedding gifts."

"Any jewelry?" Dies-Favilla inquired with more than merely a polite interest. "Gold? Silver?"

"Plenty of all three. Just bide your time, you old wurm. It'll all fall into your hoard someday anyway."

"I don't know if I have the patience to wait." The dragon's baritone chuckle shook the walls, and this time Joachim joined in.

"You know," Joachim said. "I hear that in Ingoldstadt they have nearly rebuilt the castle that was destroyed in an earthquake on a stormy night about fifteen years ago. The exact same night Gerdt woke up, I might add."

"Mmm, have they? Must be a coincidence."

"What do you have against that city, anyway?" Joachim asked.

"You mentioned the bell," the dragon said. "You understand something about love, I think."

Joachim folded his hands. Was the dragon changing the subject, or was this going somewhere? "I know a little something."

"You may find this hard to believe, Joachim, but even the black, covetous heart of a dragon can feel love, at least when it's still young. No more than two centuries old, I should say."

"And you felt love then?" Joachim asked.

"The duke of Ingoldstadt was once a formidable force in this land," Dies-Favilla went on. "He had assembled a hundred of the most courageous knights and offered a bounty on the one who could kill the scourge of the kingdom."

"You?"

"Not I," Dies-Favilla said. "I was contemptible next to this one. A female of my species. One possessed of the most terrible beauty and the fiercest appetite I have ever seen. Cities trembled when they heard the approaching rush of her wings."

The dragon was silent for a while. Joachim wondered if that was all he would get. "What was her name?" he prompted.

"You would call her…Nox-Ignis," the dragon said. "Her beauty was matched only by her recklessness. Her joy was infectious, and she spurred me to dare what I never would have on my own. Oh, the land lived in fear of us then. But eventually it caught up with us. We were raiding farms in the countryside south of Ingoldstadt one night, seeing who could roast a sheep with just one puff of breath and other such games. We must have tarried too long, for the duke and his knights arrived there to defend the farmsteads. They fired volleys of arrows, and a lucky shot struck her in a weak point."

Another silence.

"Is that when she died?" Joachim finally said.

"Not yet," Dies-Favilla said. "But the arrow drove true and injured her severely. One of the knights was able to track her to her lair. Not so difficult, really, since her dripping blood left a blazing trail behind. That man sent word back to the duke, who brought the other knights with him. They waited in stealth until I left."

"How is it you didn't sense them with your keen hearing?" Joachim asked.

"There are ways to hide yourself even from dragons, if you know," Dies-Favilla said. "The technique is not so widely known nowadays. Perhaps it's forgotten altogether. I won't share it with you."

"I didn't expect you would," Joachim said.

"So when I flew off to hunt, they crept into her lair without her knowing, and the cowards slaughtered her there, in her weakened state. And that's not all."

This time Joachim didn't interrupt the silence. He knew Dies-

Favilla would continue when he was ready.

"There…there was a hatchling there as well. *My* hatchling. Mine and Nox-Ignis's. These knights, they hacked our hatchling into a thousand pieces. And then they returned home to celebrate, toasting their deeds in the castle with ale and wine."

"What did you do?" Joachim whispered.

"When I discovered what had happened, I flew to the castle in a rage so savage only a dragon can feel it. No man could comprehend fury that deep. And I perched on a battlement of the castle and shrieked for the duke to come out, so I could look him in the eye before I killed him. He came out in his armor and offered me virgins and treasure, all to save himself, but I laughed scornfully. Finally, he offered me his most precious belonging, an artifact of true magic. You've held it in your hand."

"The bell," Joachim said.

"I took it," the dragon said, "though it did him no good."

"But after you killed him, your rage was assuaged?"

"Not at all," Dies-Favilla said. "Then I laid waste to the city so severely that no one dared return to live there for an entire generation."

Joachim blinked at that, but he pressed on. "And what did you do after that?"

"Oh, this and that. Settled here, eventually. Built up quite a lovely hoard, dispensed advice to silly villagers for hundreds of years on end. Naps. Loneliness. Ennui."

"Couldn't you take another mate, though?" Joachim asked.

"Mmm." The sound came of a huge body shifting across metal. "We were never numerous, and there aren't nearly so many of us as there used to be. Once in a great while I'll go on a flight. All night I soar, from the cold sea in the north, and over the high mountains to the warm sea in the south. Sometimes then, on the wind, I'll catch a hint of the scent of another."

"Where are they?" Joachim said.

"Holed up in some dank, secret place like me, I expect. I could investigate, even wake them. But they all smell *old*. And I am old, as well, aged almost to dust in my very bones. No, Joachim, I think the time for love has passed, for all of us. A relief for your kind, I expect."

"I feel sad for you," Joachim said.

There was silence again, and Joachim wondered if he'd gone too far.

"Convey my best wishes to Alexandra," the dragon said at last, with an air of finality.

"I will," Joachim said, taking up his lantern and turning to go. At the place where the tunnel curved, a deep sigh came from behind Joachim, wafting warm air up the passage. He had the impression the dragon was settling in to sleep for a long, long time. He started up the tunnel.

As he walked, he heard a low, rumbling tone, as if the dragon moaned or mumbled to itself. And he wasn't sure, but he thought he could even make out some words. And what he thought they said was, "Too old for love, but in the end, perhaps not quite too old…for a friend."

THE TWINS

This story has never been published anywhere before. When I read this out loud some years ago to my writers' group, the Writers of Chantilly, our native romance writer loved the erotic undertones. She called it a "fairy tale for adults," which I think is a fair way to describe it.

The twins had heard the story many times. How the porter's wife birthed them late one night in the Baron's castle. How the old cook came in to midwife and with her own hands brought the boys into the world, red and mewling. How their mother did not survive the night.

Their father spoke little, and never of the past, though many was the time they caught him looking with sadness at the old cook, only to sigh and go on with his day. But whatever grief he held in his heart, he found satisfaction in work well done and carried out his labor with dignity. Almost as soon as they could walk the boys began to help their father, carrying water from the clear stream, wooden poles over their little shoulders with five-gallon buckets hanging from each end, up the one hundred stairs shaped into the hillside, calves straining until they were carved as stone-hard as the steps.

As they grew they joined their father in other chores, and when he turned frail and aged took them over themselves: plank-broad backs rowed the supply boats across the lake and back again laden with everything the Baron's castle needed; cable-wound thighs and arms pushed the heavy casks of wine or beer or brined fish up the ramp to the cellar; knotted shoulders jerked up the lumpy 50-pound bags of potatoes or flour two at a time and bore them to the larder. The Baron's staff was not a large one and all the various heavy tasks of the household fell to the porter and his stalwart boys.

Yet the Baron was not a harsh man and the twins often had afternoons free, when they could row to the little islands dotting the lake and pass the sunny time swimming, at first with the paddle of the dog, but later after the boys in the village showed them how, with a frog's broad strokes. Or they might scale the castle walls, rising sheer from the lake's green waters, jumping out through the air and splashing into the cool murky depths when they ran out of handholds. Or wrestling, racing, throwing, and always, always competing.

One day when the boys were seventeen and vigorous in their youth, the Baron's wife looked from her window and saw them at toil in the castle courtyard, their shirts off, hoeing and shoveling the vegetable gardens, working brown and muscled under a hot sun. The Baron was an old man and she a much younger woman, and though the Baron provided her a comfortable life, he could not provide one thing she longed for.

That very night she sneaked down to the room in back the kitchen where the boys slept. Behind stone walls and heavy oaken door she taught them all she knew and much she had imagined, to their great mutual delight. The boys were fast learners and soon introduced the pretty scullery maid to their games as well, and though she was not sure it would meet the approval of the chaplain who spoke on Sundays, she did not see the harm in it.

The old cook saw much and kept her thoughts to herself as she went about her daily work. Immense and over-ripened in her age, she had once been a great beauty and even something of a lover herself, so from time to time she would have the boys row her to the Baron's forest. There she gathered a certain mushroom from the black moist earth on the north side of a great oak tree. On rainy days she added it to steaming bowls of aromatic soup she made for the Baron's wife and the scullery maid to warm them in the dank castle chambers.

But she never thought to make a bowl for the Baron's daughter, and the cook cursed herself for a fool when she realized the Baron's daughter had returned her breakfast uneaten every day for a month. A check with the laundress confirmed her suspicion. The Baron's daughter was thirteen and coming into the first bloom of her womanly beauty, and it pained the cook to think she was no longer the little girl picking flowers in the castles pleasure garden. She watched her to be sure and espied the bulge of her shame long before anybody else in the castle, and the cook knew it was time for the porter's sons to move on.

She sent a message to a cousin of hers who owned a farm some three days' distance, and as soon as she heard back, she woke the boys in the still hours and acquainted them with their mistake. They soon understood they must flee, for the Baron was not a cruel man but there were some things he certainly would not bear lightly. So the twins took the food the old cook had packed for them and followed her directions. The road was dangerous and frequented by robbers, but the boys were lucky, or perhaps it was that none dared attack the two robust-looking youths, and they reached the farm without incident.

When the merchant's wife knocked on her door in the glade, the crone knew with one look why she had come. The gray in her hair, the wrinkles in her face, the sag in those parts that had once been buoyant, and most of all the fear in her eyes that what she most dreaded was happening, little by little, but inexorably with each passing day.

"Come in, come in," the crone said. "Have a seat, my dear lady. I know just what you need."

"You do?" said the merchant's wife, sitting in a wooden chair in the crone's front room, stuffed to overflowing with drying herbs, musty books, animal furs, and crocks and pots and vessels of all sizes. "How could you know? We've never even met!"

"Oh, do not be too surprised," the crone said. "I make it my business to know the heart's desire of all who find the path to my home. I believe you have been considering this visit for some time, no?"

"Yes, I have," the merchant's wife said. "If you know all that, then you also must know I can afford to reward you handsomely, if you can help me."

"Very likely I can." The crone laughed with a rasp. "Though perhaps the price is more handsome than you anticipate."

"What do you mean? I have brought gold with me, and I can come back with more."

"Keep your gold, my lady!" the crone said. "What I ask for in payment is a favor."

"Name it."

The crone eyed the merchant's wife carefully, wondering what sort of woman she dealt with. "At the time I ask it, you must give yourself willingly to a man I shall name. That is my price."

"Oh, is that all?" the merchant's wife said, relieved her purse was not to be lightened. "I accept."

"Very good," the crone said with a yellow-toothed smile. She poked around some shelves and pulled out a tiny jar of cut glass she handed to the merchant's wife. "Take this, and spill not a drop of it. Every night before bed, you must pour a bit of it into your tea. Do this for one week."

"And that will gain me what I seek?"

"Certainly!" The rasping laugh came again. "But one more thing. Be sure you sleep alone during this week."

"I shall do so," the merchant's wife said, rising. "Thank you for your help."

"Not at all, not at all," the crone said, rasping again as she showed the lady to the door. "Farewell, until we meet again."

A few weeks later an urgent business matter required the merchant to travel, and his wife shut herself up in her chambers for the evening. After having the maidservant bring her a cup of tea, she dismissed her and bolted her door. She carefully poured in a few drops from the glass jar, sniffed it and found the acrid stench rankled her nostrils. Still she drank it down and retired for the evening.

In the middle of the night she woke feeling as if her scalp was ablaze. She fumbled to light a candle and sat at her vanity, surprised to find there appeared to be nothing wrong with her head at all. In hope it would relieve the burning sensation, she began to brush her hair. It soothed the pain, and she was delighted to find the brush pulled out the gray hairs from her head. She continued brushing throughout the night, and by the time the sun rose her hair was the same lustrous black it had been in her younger days.

Happily she went about her day's business, and that evening repeated her ritual with the tea and the drops from the jar. Again she woke in the night, this time with the feeling that thousands of insects crawled across the surface of her skin. She tried to brush them off, but her fingers detected nothing, so she lit a candle and wondered to see her skin clean. Still, the itching was unbearable, and she scratched at herself until her flesh came off in chunks and fell to the floor. Not until the sun rose did the itching end, and when she peered at herself in her vanity mirror in the early morning light, she found she had the supple smooth skin of a woman decades younger.

By the third evening she could hardly wait for the sun to go down, and again took her tea with a few drops from the jar. When she woke in the night, cramps bent her double in her bed so painfully she could barely move herself to light the candle. She fled to the garderobe where she emptied her bowels for hours. When she emerged in the morning, pale and exhausted, she hardly had the strength to carry herself back to her room. Nevertheless, she smiled when she finally saw herself in the vanity's mirror, finding her figure restored to the gracile silhouette of her teenage years.

And so it went for the rest of the week, and when the merchant returned from his journey he was astonished to find his wife of so many years looking exactly as beautiful as she had on their wedding day. He thought to ask her how this had come to be, but he was a savvy businessman and knew questioning the other side in an unexpectedly easy negotiation to be bad tactics, so he decided to simply enjoy his good fortune. The news of the miracle of the merchant's wife's beauty spread swiftly throughout the city, and older women beheld her with jealousy in the streets, and young women with awe.

For her part, the merchant's wife relished her re-found beauty as only one who has lost something precious and found it again is able. Still, she always wondered when the witch's favor would come due, until one day it did.

On the farm, the boys soon proved their worth to the cook's cousin, and it pleased him to wake early in the morning and see the luxuriant crops and fattened animals their labor had provided. The twins too found themselves happy in the challenge of hard farmwork, though the days sometimes grew monotonous on the remote homestead, so much quieter than the busy castle.

One day one of the twins weeded a spread of barley by the road while his brother worked in the barn. As he toiled, a raven-haired woman, imperious in her finery, rode by on a great black horse. She stopped where he hoed.

"What is your name, farmer boy?" she asked.

"Gabriel," he answered.

"Is it not hot for you to work in this burning sun?" she said. "Come into the road, for I have cool water here for you."

Gabriel did as she asked, and she provided him with a leather canteen. He drank deep and found the water cold and hard. He handed the canteen back, refreshed. "I thank you, my lady."

"Tell me," she said. "Do you not become lonely here on this farm, far from the nearest settlement?"

"Not at all," Gabriel answered. "I have my brother here with me, and so long as we are together we are never lonely."

"I see," the lady said, leaning down to whisper in his ear. "And yet, I think there is a sort of companionship your brother cannot provide. If I come again tonight at midnight, will you meet me by the road, and perhaps I can show you what I mean?"

Gabriel had an inkling of what the lady meant, and greatly desired it. His eyes gulped her down; he breathed in her sandalwood-laced scent. Yet he was troubled too by her request. "May I bring my brother with me?" he asked. "You see, we have always shared everything in common, even the companionship of a woman."

The lady sat back up and laughed most deliciously. "Oh, have you! I do not think so, for you are a beautiful young man, and I could hardly believe your brother could surpass you. No, you must arrive by yourself tonight."

And so that evening, the two brothers fell asleep as always on the beds of hay the farmer had provided for them in the loft of the barn. When the moon was high, Gabriel awoke and tried to sneak out of the loft, but his brother called out to him.

"Gabriel, where do you go at this hour?"

"Go back to sleep, Michael," he said. "I need only pass water." And so he left his brother and approached the road.

The lady was as good as her word and met him on her black horse. She carried him to a clearing deep in the woods where they took the pleasures of their bodies on beds of soft, sweet-smelling grass. When they were satisfied she rode him back to the farm and warned him not to tell anyone of their nighttime tryst.

And so it went for several nights. One day as they fixed a stone wall at the edge of his property, the farmer noticed Gabriel lagging at his work, barely able to keep his eyes open.

"What ails you, lad?" he asked. "I've never seen the chore you couldn't perform."

"Perhaps a touch of the grip," Gabriel said. "But I can finish here. I'll be fine."

"I don't think so, lad," the farmer said. "Off to bed with you, and in the morning you can join us if you feel better."

Gabriel trudged off, and Michael, bent over with the heft of a great stone, stared after him darkly. That evening he spoke to his brother in the dark.

"A touch of the grip," he sneered. "Maybe you took in the old man, but not me."

"I should have known you would see through me," Gabriel said.

"So tell me where you go at night."

Gabriel felt a stab of guilt for having left his brother out of his nighttime excursions, but an idea came to him that might make up for it. "Better than tell you, tonight you will come with me to the road. I will watch from a hidden place and you will take my place when the lady comes."

"The lady?"

"Wait and see," Gabriel said.

That night when the lady came by on her horse, it was Michael who was waiting for her and not Gabriel. She took him up and carried him to the spot, with Gabriel following stealthily behind. When they dismounted and the lady began to undress Michael, she stopped, puzzled. "You seem different, Gabriel. What has changed about you?"

"Nothing, my lady. Let us continue on, as usual."

"I think not," the lady said. "It is my obligation to spend the night with a certain young man, but you are not him." And she turned her back to Michael.

Michael, enraged, grabbed the lady by her arm and forced her around. "So, my brother is good enough for you but I am not, is that it?"

The lady shook her head and said, "You don't understand. It has nothing to do with you at all."

But this only angered Michael further and he struck her to the ground and raised his other fist for a second blow. At this, Gabriel leapt out from his hiding place and grabbed his brother's arm.

"Michael, what are you doing? Stop this insanity!"

Michael turned and faced Gabriel. "You! You carry on an affair with this strumpet and leave me to do all the work?"

He shoved Gabriel to the ground and picked up a large rock.

Before he could bring down the killing blow, the lady flung herself before him, sobbing. "Stop it! Stop it! I will do whatever you want, but do not harm your brother!"

Michael spat on the ground before dropping the rock. "Fine, have it your way. Run, brother. If ever I see you again, we'll continue this where we left off."

Gabriel and the merchant's wife arrived at the Baron's castle at midnight, and though the gate was closed for the night, Gabriel knew a hidden entrance requiring only a willingness to dive under the water. So the two appeared, dripping and shaking, before the old cook's room in the darkest hour. She came to her door with a candle.

"Gabriel!" She had him in her arms in an instant, all cinnamon and soap powder, but almost as quick turned on him with a reproving tongue. "What are you doing here? You know you should not be here, it is very dangerous for you. The Baron's daughter birthed her child some six months ago, and I have no doubt the Baron will have the life of whomever is responsible for his bastard grandchild."

"I know, Nana," Gabriel said. "I had no choice, for Michael and I have quarreled, and he swore to kill me if ever he lays eyes on me again."

"Michael and you have quarreled?" the cook said in amazement, before narrowing her eyes at the merchant's wife, taking in her fine features and ample bosom. "Well, I suppose I can guess the cause of it. But never mind that, get you in my chamber and I'll build a fire before the two of you freeze."

The cook gave them her bed for the night and left for they knew not where, but they heard her in the kitchen before dawn beginning her work for the day, preparing the breakfast and the other meals as well. When the scullery maid came in at her usual time, the cook told her she was leaving for a few days and the maid would have to take over the cooking duties.

"But what about washing the dishes? The pots and pans? And

all the rest of it? Am I to do two jobs?"

"You'll manage," the old cook said. "And I've left a note explaining things to the steward. He'll understand. I'll be back as soon as I can."

And with that, she was off down the stairs to a waiting rowboat, where Gabriel and the merchant's wife sat in hooded robes. The precaution was probably unnecessary in the foggy early morning but the cook insisted upon it. Gabriel rowed and when they reached the far side of the lake, they were relieved to find the lady's horse still tied up where they had left it the night before.

They started on their way and made good time, with Gabriel a strong walker and the ladies alternating riding on the horse. The closer they came to the farm, the greater Gabriel's apprehension grew, until as they walked he confessed to the cook the entire story of his affair with the merchant's wife and his brother's vow to kill him. The merchant's wife tried at times to shush him, but he continued on, eager to get the secret out in the open.

"I thought it was something of the sort," was all the old cook said when he finished, and she continued to lead the way with nary a look back at the other two.

At the end of the third day, they stopped at a place where a side path diverged from the main route. Gabriel was surprised when they took the path, for he had not seen it from the road. Perhaps it had been hidden by some trick of light or untidy undergrowth. Moreover, they were not far from the farm, so it was not clear what need they had to stop at whatever woodcutter's cottage to which this led. He sensed the lady stiffen on the horse behind him.

"Must we stop here, good cook?" the lady called as she rode. "There is an inn not far. If we are to stop and spend the night, I can cover the cost."

"No, this is the way we must take," the old cook said. They soon came to a large house, although in such a state of disrepair it looked as if it might tumble down in the next big rainstorm. The cook strode to the front door, rapping with her walking stick. The door opened a crack and an old crone peeked out.

"Raye," the cook said. "Open this door immediately."

"Why, Faye," the crone said, slowly opening it a bit further. "Is that any way to greet your sister?" She spotted Gabriel and the merchant's wife in her front garden. "Ah, and you've brought guests! Well, if you've traveled all this way I suppose you should all come in."

The three filed into the crone's overstuffed sitting room. "I know the lady of course," she said, giving a slight nod. "Madame is as beautiful as ever. Even more, I think, than the last time I saw her." She let out a dry cackle. "But the young man I have not met."

"My name is Gabriel, ma'am," he said, extending his hand.

"Yes, of course it is," the crone said. "How silly of me not to remember."

"I'm sorry?" Gabriel said. "Do you know me from somewhere?"

There was a noise from the door to the next room and the three guests turned to see. Michael filled the doorway, holding a heavy hickory branch in one hand. He stabbed angry glowering eyes at Gabriel and the merchant's wife.

"So, the old lady was right. I don't know how she knew, but she said you were coming back, brother. And you've brought the whore you've taken up with as well."

"I…I didn't know you'd be here, Michael," Gabriel said. "It is good to see you, no matter what you may think."

Michael laughed. "I have learned the true story, my brother, of our parentage."

"Michael," the old cook said. "Whatever she told you—"

"Shut up, woman!" Michael shouted at her. He turned his attention back to Gabriel. "Everything we've ever been told is a lie. I think you'll be quite interested to hear the truth. I shall explain it to you as your life's blood runs into the ground, so you'll know what a fool you've been."

He lunged at Gabriel, driving Gabriel to the ground in a crunch of cracking wood and crockery. Surprise had given Michael the initiative, but Gabriel had grappled with his brother constantly since they could walk and soon had him flipped over.

At the same time the crone lifted a jar filled with pink powder from a shelf and flung its contents at her sister. The pink granules grew, becoming demonic little biting jaws as they flew in the air. The cook, anticipating some sort of trickery, herself reached in a bag tied to her waist and drew out a handful of glowing fireflies which she spread in a wave around herself. A shimmering shield solidified among the insects and the pink biting jaws bounced harmlessly against it, dropping to the floor where they chattered off into the cobwebbed corners of the room.

The merchant's wife could hardly make sense of the carnage unfolding in the room and hurled herself through the nearest window with a shriek without even bothering to open it. She landed in a pile of leaves outside the house, not noticing the blood flowing from the many places the shattered glass had cut her skin. She jumped atop her horse and rode straight for the farmhouse.

The twins wrestled each other through the house, shaking the floors and walls with their blows and falls, splintering furniture and toppling bookcases. Their struggle took them up and down stairs, through bedrooms and hallways, across the crossbeams in the attic until they fell into the room below in a heap of powder and debris, amid the barrels and crates of the basement which they flung aside in their struggle. Each strike deflected, every grab for a limb futile, each thrust of a knee or elbow dodged in time, and even after hours neither could find an advantage.

As the boys wrestled the crone and the cook flung potions and powders at each other, dodging and running and screaming incantations, searching the crannies of the house for spiders or mice or molds to sacrifice for their hexes. Spells lit the house and burst out the windows with multi-colored explosions like fireworks, others crept along the floorboards like malevolent shadows, seeking a victim to strangle. Some settled into walls that grew grasping arms or floors that opened with gaping maws.

Finally the twins tumbled out the front door and down the steps to the bare ground where they lay entwined, sweaty and gasping but neither giving in. The old women stumbled out after them only moments later, facing each other with bloodshot eyes.

But here the crone saw her chance, for a gnarled old pine tree rose behind Gabriel at the edge of the wood. She leaped to the top step and gestured at the giant tree. It bent its top to the ground. The crone released the tree with an opening of her fingers and the spring-drawn trunk whipped towards the house. The cook, who had been readying another attack, saw out of the corner of her eye what was about to happen, and used the last of her strength to jump across and knock Gabriel out of its path. The strain of the whiplash was too much even for the mighty trunk, and the tree snapped in half, driving its tip through Michael and impaling him against the outer wall of her house.

The house shuddered and clouds of dust wafted out the broken windows. The crone laughed from where she perched at the top of the stairs.

"You couldn't do it Faye!" she cackled. "You couldn't save both of them! A son dead, and my promise fulfilled." With a final hoarse laugh, the blood drained from the crone's face and she collapsed, crumpling down the steps. The old cook rose from where she and Gabriel had hit the ground and ran to her.

"Raye, can you hear me?"

The crone did not answer. The cook put her ear to her sister's mouth and felt no breath on her cheek.

"Is she dead?" Gabriel asked.

The old cook nodded. "She must have used the very last of her breath for that final trick."

They both sat against the side of the beaten-down house,

exhausted, filthy, blood-spattered, stale sweat and dust in their eyes and throats.

"I would weep had I a drop of moisture left in my body," the old cook croaked.

Gabriel spotted a well in the wood and fetched them water to drink, carrying it back with a bowl he found flung out a window.

The old cook drank slowly and rested a moment before speaking. "No, even with water I have no tears."

"Nor do I, Nana. Maybe I will later."

"I suppose I should have told you a long time ago."

Gabriel put a hand on the cook's arm. "Don't speak, Nana. Conserve your strength so we can walk out of here."

"My life is ebbing, and there is nothing to be done," she said. "I knew this day would come and prepared for it. Now that it is finished I am truly spent. But before I die, I wish you to know the true story."

Gabriel shook his head. "You don't need to tell me anything. I know the witch was full of lies and tricks. How else could she make my brother hate me so?"

"She may well have done," the old cook said. "But lies need a kernel of truth to be believed. Will you listen?" She took his hand.

"If you must speak, Nana, my ears are open."

The old cook breathed in, deep and rattling. "Raye and I, we were like you and Michael, born one after the other. From our mother we learned the arts of healing, of the herbs and roots and leaves of the forest. But we learned more than that, as well, things our mother suspected but in her wisdom never delved into. But we dared, my sister and I! In our youthful bravado we studied things beyond our mother's ken, traveled dark and forbidden paths, and became arrogant in our knowledge. I was content merely to *learn* the secret ways, but Raye, she wanted more. And what she could do became known throughout the land." She coughed and droplets of blood sprayed her hand.

"Stop, Nana, you don't have the strength!"

She held up a hand and closed her eyes, opened them again with force of will. "Gabriel, you must know. Your father is no porter. He was once one of the Baron's knights, in a day when the Baron's authority and protection extended far and one could travel in these parts without fear. But the Baron stripped him of his knighthood and his glory after a great shame."

"My father? A great shame?"

She nodded. "Your father took my sister as his bride. In those times, she was icy and beautiful. Many men desired her, but it was your father who won her, not knowing the ice went right down to her heart. Your father was a good man on the day they wed, but she bent him, in time turning his honor to ambition and his goodwill to malice. With her at his side, he became the greatest of the Baron's knights, but the cruelest. He rode the countryside, taking what he wanted. And one night, what he wanted was me."

Gabriel's face turned to horror. "But I can hardly believe this Nana. My father is the mildest of men. How can it be so?"

"Age, my son, has ways to humble and gentle the wildest beast. But in those days your father was brash and handsome and charming and I gave myself to him, wholly and willingly. And perhaps I wanted a little of what my sister had achieved, after all. But do not think my feelings were false. I loved him then, and I love him still. It was not long until I was with child. When my sister learned of this, you can imagine her rage.

"In her fury she brought plague upon the Baron's household, and he drove her out. But before she fled, she promised her vengeance on me. None but me ever knew she remained in the Baron's realm, secreted in this hidden cranny. I suppose she had been waiting for her opportunity all these years."

The coughing took the old cook again, and this time Gabriel did not tell her to stop. When it passed she went on. "If things turned out happier than they might have, it is only because of the kindness of the Baron. Despite his disgrace, the Baron remembered all the valiant services your father had performed for him, and permitted him to stay on as a porter at the castle. He found a place there, too, for your father's lover, me. As for my children, they were to be raised within the castle walls, with no mention ever to be made of the shameful circumstances of their birth. I could raise you as a mother, but no one would ever know I actually was so."

In the morning, the merchant's wife arrived on her black horse with the farmer walking beside her. They found Gabriel scooping the last shovelfuls of dirt onto a makeshift grave. He had built a small cairn of rocks at the head of it and his eyes were red with grief.

"Who do you bury here, Gabriel?" the farmer asked him.

"My brother, sir. And my mother. And my aunt."

"I wondered what happened to the both of you, gone now these many days," the farmer said. He glanced at the ruined house, groaning with the damage from the fight. "What foul business passed here?"

"Foul indeed, as you say," Gabriel said. "A quarrel, between my brother and me, that I understand little. And another, older one, that I understand even less. Searching my conscience, I can't say I should have done anything different."

The farmer was silent for a time. "I did not favor my cousins' way of life. A lot of trouble, from all I ever heard of them. Still, I was always rather fond of Faye. I offer you my condolences."

Gabriel only nodded.

The farmer said, "You and your brother left me in a spot when you departed so suddenly. Will you come back with me to the farm?"

"I am sorry," Gabriel said. "But I am heart-sore. Returning there would bring back too many memories."

"Where will you go?" the merchant's wife asked him.

"I do not know," he answered.

"Then come with me," she said. "My husband is a rich man with many business interests. I am sure he can find a place for you."

Gabriel tossed his shovel to the side. "Let us go, my lady. I do not wish to stay here a moment longer."

The return of the merchant's wife swung a household in mourning to one in celebration. The day she arrived, the merchant held a feast in her honor that very evening. He invited all the right people, said all the right things, called for the finest wines from his cellar. But a coldness in his manner and steel in his eyes showed his wife all was not well.

At the close of the evening, as the gentlemen and ladies stood chatting, she approached him at a moment he stood alone. She put her hand on his arm and he drew back.

"My husband, are you not glad to see me? Days I have spent fearing for my life in the clutches of ruffians, not knowing if I would ever be with you again."

But the merchant only sipped his brandy and nodded his head at Gabriel, lurking awkward in a corner of the room. "I wonder about your rescuer," he said. "Did he really fight the kidnappers, or was he on their payroll?" And a further suspicion as well, unvoiced, but he knew his wife's loveliness drew the attention of many men.

"Hans, don't be like that! He helped me escape with no thought of the danger to himself."

"Is that so?"

"Yes!" his wife said. "He overpowered the guard at the basement door, and when the others set upon him, he fought them off as well."

"Did he now?" the merchant said. Her story felt rehearsed, but he sensed the eyes of the townspeople on him, ready to spread gossip if there were even a hint of strife in the family. And in any case, his wife was back, and as beautiful as ever, though covered with cuts and scratches. So he took her in his arms, and later held his hand out to Gabriel as well, offering him thanks without sincerity.

The next morning he discreetly sent a servant to check on the remote spot his wife had described as the ruffians' house. As for the young man she had brought home, he put him to work at his warehouse by the river. The job of loading and unloading the boats docked there was not for the weak of back, but this boy seemed he might get on.

The servant returned a few days later and reported the house was abandoned though recently occupied, and showed signs of an epic struggle. The merchant began to consider that maybe his wife was telling the truth, if not quite all of it. He had often warned her off from walking by herself outside the town gate, but she had always been high-spirited and disposed to obstinance. He supposed she simply did not want to admit he had been right all along. Well, he saw no gain in wounding her pride further by pressing the matter.

As for the young man, he had already proved himself of more than a little help. Indeed, his unstinting work ethic had done much to allay the merchant's suspicions. The manager at the warehouse could not speak highly enough of him, claiming it was his efforts that had cleared the backlog of crates and barrels on the merchant's wharf for the first time in months.

"Perhaps he is as good a fellow as my wife says," he thought to himself. "But let us examine the wares before receiving them."

Thus it was he invited Gabriel to dine at their table a few weeks later. Gabriel was not accustomed to eating sauce-laden rich foods nor with silver table settings, and spent an uncomfortable hour, especially when the merchant asked him if he knew his niece, Donella, and if so, did he find her pretty? Gabriel, now truly sweating, admitted he had met her, and thought she was pretty enough. This was something of a fib, for the dark-eyed and feisty girl had attracted his attention from the first time he'd seen her, and though she was surprised when he appeared in her room one evening after the house was quiet, had willingly invited him into her bed and on many nights thereafter.

The merchant, for his part, saw Gabriel's inelegance and

found it fitting for a hard-working young man not to be too familiar with luxury, and took his unease about Donella for shyness. Though the young man derived of lowly parentage, still he had served in the Baron's castle, and that could be an advantage. Having no children of his own, the merchant even entertained the notion that Gabriel might make a suitable candidate to take over the trade someday.

After the meal the merchant asked Gabriel if he would like Donella's hand in marriage. With some relief at where the line of questioning had ended up, Gabriel agreed readily, and Donella squealed with unladylike joy when her aunt, the merchant's wife, came to her with the proposal.

The wedding took place a month hence, the bride resplendent in her white dress, the groom itchy in his ill-fitting finery, the aunt and uncle proud. Even the old Baron showed up, much to the surprise of all, but he had always been fond of the twins, perhaps still feeling a lick of guilt about their father's sad fate, and anyway regretted they had left his service the previous year so suddenly and mysteriously. Such a fine young man, too bad he was below his daughter's station, for the sons of the noblemen in the region were cads to the last man and given to taking the honor of young women. As if a thirteen-year-old girl were a mere flower to be plucked, and in his own home as well! The Baron shook himself of his bitter reverie in time to give his blessing to the young couple and bade them visit the castle from time to time.

And at the altar, Donella smiled, for only that morning she had felt the first stirrings of new life inside her. But what even she did not know was that there was not one child in her belly, but two.

MOUNTAIN MAN

This story first appeared in the 2020 Writers of Chantilly anthology, Hindsight. *It was inspired by a trip I took to a historic salt mine in Poland when I was an exchange student in Germany during college. The mine was no longer active, but had been worked for centuries. We climbed down a wooden staircase so tall that you could not its bottom or top as you descended. The mine was cool and musty in some parts, warm in others. As we visited the various chambers, I gradually got the distinct impression it was a living, breathing space, a feeling I never forgot.*

It was our fathers who heard it first. Almost imperceptible in the beginning, more a slight, momentary rise in air pressure than a sound. Later, as weeks and years passed, it grew stronger, a definite sudden vibration in the ground, rising up into the soles of the feet and through the body, and then gone almost as soon as it'd started. Grew more frequent, too. Decades ago, maybe once a week, but by now every day.

As we descended the wooden staircase with lanterns in hand, descending so far down you could not see the bottom or the top, just the lanterns bobbing in a vertical line in the dark, we would argue about what it was. "An underground river," one man said, "and someday the water will burst through and wash us all away, tools and carts and men and everything, with no more mercy but the grave."

I had another opinion. "Sounds like no river I ever heard. More like a drum. I think maybe there's somebody down below, digging like us, only coming up instead of going down, and one fine day we'll meet them and we'll see how the people in the center of the world look."

A few laughed at that, but most kept their silence, for we were deep now and the mine was not altogether different from a chapel, or a tomb, and as you entered it a natural reverence tended to take over. In that place, the pick-axes rang like bells, and a shout had been known to bring down ceilings, so most avoided speaking above a murmur except in an emergency.

I was with my gang as we carved out a new seam that had only been discovered a few days before, almost unbelievable in its purity, a virgin vein of real anthracite with no clay and hardly any slate, each blow bringing out cascades of coal, hard and black and pure. We'd make ten tons apiece today, easy, and that meant money, maybe fifteen *groszy* for the week. We'd follow the vein until it played out. If we were lucky it might last weeks, and we could earn half a year's pay in a single month.

I stood with the lantern and watched Aleksy, the gang leader, stripped to his waist despite the cool damp air, back muscles rippling with each swing of the pick-axe and sweat running from his hair down his torso, leaving white paths in the coal dust that coated his skin. I thought the men looked beautiful underground, muscles hard as the rock and skins dark as the shadow. I suppose other men felt the same way, but if they did we never spoke of it. After Aleksy reached his limit, I handed the lantern to the man behind me and took my turn. The work felt good, early in the morning still, the axe tip bouncing once, twice, and the third impact pulverizing, sweeping through the imploded stone.

As I went on, three feet, four, keeping the shovelmen busy filling the cart, the wall started to feel strange. Wet, somehow, or spongy, and the rubble didn't fall brittle but soft. I glanced back at one point at one of the shovelmen, Jurek, but if he noticed anything wrong his face didn't betray it, so I kept at it, until one final swing broke through, and black liquid oozed out from the hole. I dropped the pick-axe then, and the man with the lantern stepped forward.

"What is it?" Jurek asked, discarding his shovel and crowding around with the others. Gallons flowed out in huge round drops, gooping thickly onto the floor.

I put a finger in and drew it out. Warm and sticky. I sniffed the residue, and it was no different than the normal wet-rock smell. "Smells like coal."

"I've never seen it like that," one man said. "Is it safe?"

"Only dangerous if it's gas," Aleksy said. "Get back to work."

"Can't go farther here," I said. "This isn't rock. Can't pick it."

"We'll see about that." Aleksy hefted the pick-axe and took a huge swing, but it only created another opening for the oozing black coal, which by now was puddling around our boots. "Damn it," he said. And we all knew why, because that was *kopeks* we wouldn't be earning.

When you spend your days underground the full moon may as well be the noonday sun, and I found myself that night sitting in a chair by the window, listening to the slow breathing of Marta in our bed and the fast breathing of little Karol in his crib. Outside, the other houses lay quiet and the mountain rose up hard just past the village boundary, the silver birches growing in little clumps where they could find purchase, but large parts of the face only steep, bare rock, all rising to the strange white crown of stone ringing the mountain's summit. Stary Blondyn, we called the mountain—old blondie. My eyes followed our little trail up to the collar of the mine entrance, a tiny scratch on the face ending in a pimple.

Marta must have sensed my disquiet and stirred. "Piotrek, what is wrong? Come back to bed."

I took one last look at Stary Blondyn and slid back under the quilt, slipping my hand around her hip, bringing her close to me.

"What do you think about at the window?" she whispered, so I told her of the strange event at the mine that day.

"I don't like it," she said. "It's unnatural. Perhaps you dig too deep."

"Perhaps," I said. "But we must, for that is where the coal remains, and we have to follow where the coal leads."

I think she was about to say something more but Karol cried out in his sleep. We did not speak then, but waited for the baby to settle. Marta's face was clean and white in the moonlight and when I kissed her cheek, traced my fingers across her body and over her breast, she did not turn away. After our lovemaking finished I finally fell asleep.

The next day, the entire tunnel had filled with the liquid coal and even spilled as far as the crosscut. In a few weeks, we had to close off the whole section. Nor was that the last time it happened. The next occasion was about a year later, not our gang this time, but from what I heard the circumstances were the same. A rich new vein of pure black anthracite, progress accelerated by the men's eagerness to profit, but stopped suddenly with an inflow of viscous warm liquid.

And again a few months after that, and a few months after that as well, and with greater frequency over the years so that eventually large parts of the mine, hewn out so carefully over the centuries by our grandfathers and their grandfathers, now became inaccessible. Tunnel after tunnel, shaft after shaft, lost to the advancing flood tide. Increasingly, we were pressed back to the upper tunnels, where all that remained to mine was the lignite, the brown coal that smoked terribly when burned, and brought only sparse wages for twelve hours of hard labor.

The quality of the air in the mine changed too. Where once it had been cool and still, now the atmosphere turned warm, even sultry. Where once trickles of sweat had made snakes in the coal dust down men's torsos, now the rivulets of sweat washed the dust away, soaking pants and leaving axe handles hard to grip. And the air moved now too, not the gentle ventilation drafts through the upcast shafts, but great pressure waves gusting first down the tunnels and then back up, as if the mountain itself were squeezing and releasing.

And the thumping, which so many decades ago had been the first sign, now every hour, the drum-like vibration humming through the tunnel ribs, powerful enough to upend carts. Of course the fear was eventually that one would be powerful enough to collapse the timbers in some tunnel or shaft, burying miners under tons of rock, or even worse, stranding them underground in some dark tunnel with no hope of escape. But miners live with that fear every day, so we kept working. There was nothing else to do.

One Sunday, coming home after the service in our little village church, Marta said to me as ten-year-old Karol walked ahead of us out of earshot, "I hope for a different life for him."

"What do you mean?"

"There is no future here," she said. "Look at the village. We can no longer afford the things we used to."

I nodded. It was true. A week's wages at the mine used to purchase decent clothes, furnishings for our homes, new roofs, thriving taverns. Well, the taverns were still left, anyway, full of sullen men worried if they could afford enough potatoes and turnips to feed their families until the end of the month. The once white-washed walls of the village's buildings now showed a shabby brown, covered in the greasy ash from burning lignite for heat and light.

"But where could we go?" I asked. "What else could I do?"

"We could move to the city," Marta said. "They say there are many jobs there for a man."

"Maybe," I said. I tried to imagine the city. So many buildings and people in every direction it stretched to the horizon, people said. So many people you could never meet them all in a hundred years. "How would we get there? Where would we stay?"

"I've got a little money saved," Marta said. "We could live for a time."

I raised my eyebrows. Marta had never told me she was saving money. And despite the low wages I'd brought home in the past months—she was a wonder! "Well. How much money do you have then?"

"Enough." She glanced ahead at Karol, now talking to another boy his age he'd met on the road. "For a few months."

"And suppose I didn't find a job? What would we do when your savings ran out? It would be a cold, hungry winter."

"It could be cold and hungry here if things don't improve."

She had a point there. For some reason I remembered a story I'd heard once, as a kid, from a peddler passing through. He'd had a strange way of speaking, said he'd lived on the sea far to the south, a place that never felt the cold crack of wind in winter, and trees in the gardens were full of fruit. I'd hardly known whether to believe him. It seemed if such a place were real, nobody would ever want to leave, yet here he was in our village, selling his tin goods. I asked him why he was here and not there, and he said he was saving his *kopeks* to return someday.

Even now, it seemed hard to believe such stories. All that was real in this world was the mountain, the mine, the village. My grandfather had lived his whole life here, and I doubt his own grandfather was any different. Centuries stretched into the past and would continue to stretch into the future. And even if there were such a place as the peddler had described, no matter, for I knew it was not for the likes of me.

And then it happened. We were on scaling duty on that day, all of us with shovels except Aleksy in the front with the slate bar, scraping the loose waste material left behind after mining from the ceilings and ribs. Gangs hated to do it because it didn't pay, but every gang had to do it one day a week. It was necessary work to prevent dangerous falls of unexpected material, and thoroughness was required.

The atmosphere was thick and humid, almost hard to breathe, and the thumps, every quarter hour now, reverberated through the tunnel like the air in a drum. Now came a big thump, the most powerful one yet, rattling our ribcages and the tunnel walls, and then a sound like something shifting in the rock above us. I looked up to see the timber crossbars on the ceiling bending under some new weight, and one by one, the pinnings popped out, hitting the floor with ringing metallic pings. I started running but too late, the crossbars gave way, and it all came in, rock falling like a summer rainstorm.

Somehow it took both a long time and only a few moments, all at once, and when the rock and dust settled it was completely dark. I coughed and it sounded far away. At least I could breathe, that was good. I felt around with my hands. I was buried up to my waist in rubble. One leg I could feel, one I couldn't. There were patches on my skull and shoulder that were wet, but if they were wounds I couldn't tell at first. The pain only came later.

Aleksy's voice came to me as if shouting from miles away, though he had been right beside me when the cave-in started. "Rollcall!" it called faintly.

"Piotrek *tutaj*!" I answered.

"Marek *tutaj*!"

"Jurek *tutaj*!"

"Janusz *tutaj*!"

"Stefan *tutaj*!"

Incredibly all six in the gang were accounted for, not a single loss. We went around again, describing our injuries as best we could. Jurek was the worst—it seemed he was crushed under a fallen timber and could not take in a full breath.

If we had thought the worst of the ordeal was over, though, we were wrong, for it was only the beginning. Over the next hours my hearing gradually returned but so did the feeling in my left leg, and I soon realized the bones must be broken. The deep pain made me want to scream but I did not, for others in the tunnel were in worse shape. I had to be calm for them.

In the dark we called out to each other from time to time. We told each other stories and thoughts. Wishes to our see our families, go home for dinner. Not many jokes. I suppose we slept. Hunger came and went again. We could tell the passing of time from the number of thumps, or rather, we could have if we'd been counting correctly. By Janusz's count it had been three days, by Aleksy's only a day and a half.

That was about when Jurek stopped answering. The rest of us wondered how soon until we would follow—perhaps the next thump would be the one to finish the cave-in. Or, just as likely, we would run out of air, eventually. Maybe that way would be better. Just go to sleep, ending the pain. It seemed to me we were sleeping more already. But maybe it was only from boredom, or from having run out of things to talk about.

We heard tapping, on either day four (Janusz) or day two (Aleksy). Our air was definitely running low. There was little talk and when we did, our words came out silly. It was hard to think clearly. Things struck us as funny for no reason at all. Sometimes I would fall asleep laughing and laugh again when I woke from my nap. The tapping grew louder. Would they reach us in time? That was funny too.

They did, and the cold air hit our skin like a slap in the face. Five survivors, three days trapped underground. For a short time we were heroes in the village, though I'm not sure why. We'd done what we had to, nothing more. My crushed leg was useless. The doctor broke it again so it would heal straight, if it did heal. As for infection, I was lucky. It would have set in already if it was going to, and it hadn't. Stefan was not so lucky, and ended up with a leg cut off below the knee.

I did not return to the mine. How could I, with my leg? The others did, as soon as they healed. Well, not Stefan. There was a fund for men like Stefan and me, although I hated to take the money. But I had no choice.

Other men in my situation spent their days drinking at the tavern. Not me. I sat at the window of my home. I grumbled a lot, but mostly watched. People walked by. Birds, animals. Stary Blondyn stood tall past the houses. The autumn came, the leaves fell, nights grew cold, then mornings and evenings as well, and the cold seeped into my leg and fed the pain. Only in the afternoons did it ease a bit, and I could maybe sleep for a couple hours. The hours before dawn were the worst, and as I looked out the window at the mountain, biting my lip and eyes tearing, it almost seemed sometimes as if the mountain trembled, a quick shake, just a bit. But I would blink the water away and of course everything was in its same place, where it should be. Had been forever, and always would be.

Marta was good, much better to me than I was to her. "When you're healthy again," she said, "I think we should move. Like we spoke of before. If you can't work in the mine again, there must surely be a place in the city for a man who will work hard."

"Don't be stupid," I said. "Why would the city want a lame man any more than the mine does? I'll die here like I was born here."

Off she'd go then, on her errands in the village, visiting with her friends. As the winter went on, my leg did heal, slowly, at first only so I could walk from my chair to the bed, and after I'd mastered that, I practiced walking around our house. By March I even ventured out into the street once a day, for ten minutes, then fifteen. And as the world warmed, the pain was less, during the day at least. But when evening fell the pain returned.

I was at the window one night in April, another full moon like on a previous night so long ago, with Marta asleep, and Karol too, now practically a young man, snoring in his bed. My leg throbbed as I sat, and I kneaded my thigh with my hands, providing some temporary relief as I stared out at the unmoving mountain.

Except, tonight, it did move. A slight shudder in the white stone crown at the summit. I blinked my eyes, but no water was in them this time. Surely a trick, though, probably from lack of sleep. But it happened again, this time across the whole mountain, a tremor, accompanied by a cracking sound that didn't stop. Two huge rock humps, one on either side of the crown, rose out of the mountain, sending boulders bouncing down the face, knocking over huge birches like twigs crunching under your boot.

"What is it?" Marta murmured from bed. "Is something happening?"

"Nothing," I said. "Go back to sleep."

But I continued to watch, as the two humps rose farther, lifting the entire mountain with them, pushing up until there was a gap where the mountain had been, supported by huge stone pillars. The humps looked for all the world like…shoulders, and the pillars like arms. Arms, with rock fists braced against the ground, thrusting up until the whole mountain was in the air, hundreds of feet high, and it swung itself out of its hole, dust falling from the sky in clouds.

I ignored my throbbing leg and climbed out the window so I could see better, rubbed the dust from my face, and there was the mountain, with those pillars at its side, and two more underneath, and those pillars underneath extended themselves until they reached the ground. They took a step, and then another, and stopped. The pillars at the sides reached out, one down and one up, akimbo, the body of the mountain arching, as if it was stretching, working out the kinks. The white crown at the top turned one way and then the other, maybe taking a good look at the landscape. And then the bottom pillars stepped again, and this time they didn't stop but kept walking, to the south.

I watched until the mountain was out of sight, and the dust settled, and where before Stary Blondyn had loomed up over the village there was now only black starry sky. And I understood in that moment something I had not before. Things can seem permanent, but in a moment they can shift before you know it.

In the morning the village awoke to the change in the landscape. Men and women came out of their houses and wailed in the streets, and the priest shouted that it was a sign from God and we should repent, for He would be coming soon. I kissed Marta and told her to pack our things, whatever we might need for a journey. Clothes, our family Bible, the money she had saved. Any little things she or Karol might want to keep.

"But why? Where are we going, Piotrek?"

"Go and look out the window," I said. She gasped when she saw.

Soon we were making our way through the village, our belongings gathered in bundled sheets tied at the end and hung from broomstick handles we carried over our shoulders. The sun had risen and its rays spilled through the new gap, pouring light over our town a full hour before we normally saw it. Neighbors we'd known for years as sober drank vodka openly, and the priest by now had organized a train of men and women, chanting prayers and fingering rosaries behind him while he carried a cross high and marched around the town's central square.

As we walked I heard snatches of conversation, shouts and murmurs, trying to explain what had happened. "An earthquake," one man claimed. "A perfectly scientific explanation."

"No, you fool," another shouted. "The hand of God reached down and plucked out Stary Blondyn to punish us for our wickedness, just like Sodom and Gomorrah."

I smiled to myself. Only I had seen what had really happened, and no one would believe me if I explained it.

We strolled along the road out of the village. It led eventually from the mountains to the land of green rolling hills beyond, or so I'd heard, as I'd never myself been down it more than ten miles. I hoped to be farther than that by the end of the day. My leg felt curiously healthy. Outside the village things were peaceful, hawfinches peeping their quiet songs and siskins twittering their brighter ones in the birch trees.

"What has happened, Father?" Karol asked me. "Was it really the hand of God that took the mountain?"

"No, it wasn't the hand of God," I said. I thought back on all the things that had happened in the mine. The thumping. The flowing black coal, which nobody had ever seen before. It struck me that we had been cleaning out the man in the mountain.

Shoveling out his veins and arteries of the hard coal that blocked them, clearing the way for his black blood to pump. Scraping out the lignite deposited in his head that kept his thoughts from working. Tiny little doctors we'd been, in a way. But how could I ever tell anyone what I'd seen last night, even my own family? They'd think I'd lost my mind for sure.

"So it was an earthquake, then," Marta said.

"Not that either," I said. "The mountain decided it was time to go and he went, that's all. He went to the south, to where it's warmer. And that's where we shall go as well."

"But where?" Karol asked. "Where exactly are we going?"

I considered a moment before answering. It didn't have to be the same, always. You could fall asleep in one place for centuries, only to awaken and leave when the notion took ahold of you. "A new place," I said. "A place near the sea where it will be warm the whole year, and we'll have trees in our garden from which we can pick fruit whenever we want."

LA JOLLA BALLROOM

La Jolla Ballroom *first appeared in the 2017 Writers of Chantilly anthology,* Soundtracks of our Lives. *I had found a website with a really cool list of 1930s and 40s slang and just started playing around with that. I had also recently taken a trip to my company's headquarters in La Jolla, California, and drank in a beachside scotch bar very similar to the one described in the story. Somehow the two came together easily and beautifully. This is my mother's favorite story of mine, by the way.*

I put an elbow on the mahogany bar slab, lifted a finger to signal the bartender.

"Another Oban, sir?" he asked me.

"Please," I said.

The bar was close enough to the ocean to hear the waves, soothing background noise accompanied by clinking glasses and murmured voices. A warm nighttime breeze filled the room with a gentle salty tang, a fine complement to the smoky, peaty scotches the place specialized in. It was almost enough to make me forget the credit card bills, the late mortgage payment, the bookies on my back. Almost.

An old man in a tuxedo took the empty bar stool beside me. "The regular, Jimmy," he said in a voice so graveled he could've laid a driveway with it. The bartender brought him a glass filled almost to the top. "What's this?" the old man asked.

"Your regular, sir," Jimmy said.

"Wonderful place, this." The man smiled at me and took a sip. "Never seen you around before."

"Here for a conference," I said. "Couldn't resist a bar on the beach."

"La Jolla's great that way," the old man said. He took another sip. Though worn in the elbows and fraying at the sleeves, his double-breasted jacket was still as elegant as it must have been decades earlier, and his two-tone shoes were shined to lacquered perfection.

"You coming back from a party?" I asked.

"No, going to one," he said. "The night is still young, right?"

"Of course." I bet this guy had a lot of stories. Old guys in bars usually do. "You meeting a date there?"

"Ha! Sure am." He gave me a wink. "The most beautiful girl in the world, in fact. How about you? Young good-looking fella like you must have a steady girlfriend."

"Not at the moment, I'm afraid," I said. A lie. Not sure why I did it, but it seemed harmless in the moment. Looking back, I think that's where things started to go a little crazy.

"You'd better come with me, then," he said. "There'll be plenty of dolls where I'm headed."

"I don't know, I have to get up pretty early for the conference tomorrow morning."

"Forget about that," he said. "Here's my advice: you can't live if you don't lose a little sleep." He clinked his glass on the counter, drained to the bottom. "I'm going, if you want to come along. It's not too far. A short walk won't wear you out, will it?"

"All right." I finished my own glass in a hurry. "You talked me into it."

The walk truly was short—he went to the door at the end of the bar. I half-expected it would open onto a broom closet and prove the old fellow senile, but no, beyond was a stairway going down. I followed him across the threshold.

A sudden cold wind gusted in from the ocean. I shivered as the chill snaked down my back. Reminded me of back home, gray and snowy and dull all winter, even through March. Snowed two inches the day before I'd left, just in time for the evening rush home. On top of that, the last night before flying out I'd had another money argument with Stephanie. The bills were piling up fast, I had to admit, but I sure as hell didn't need it thrown in my face how much I'd gambled away. So I'd been on a losing streak, so what? She hadn't exactly slowed down her spending when our bank accounts bottomed out.

I'd tried to interest her in making love before bed, but she wasn't having it. Too tired. Well, I was tired too. Tired of it all. God, this week in California was just what I needed.

"You'd better close that door behind you," the old man said.

I shook my head, my reverie broken. "Right," I said, and did so.

At the bottom we pushed through a set of double doors and emerged into an elegant old ballroom, the kind that just isn't built anymore. It must have been some sort of theme night because everyone was dressed to the nines: men in tuxedoes, women in knee-length dresses and curled hair. On the stage a big band played a foxtrot, their brass instruments gleaming in the light of a huge chandelier. A few couples danced, but my friend nudged me and nodded in the direction of the bar.

"Two scotches," he said to the bartender.

As soon as he spoke, a woman in an emerald green dress looked up from a nearby table. "Porter?" she said. If her hair was any redder it would have been on fire, if her eyes were any greener they would have been the sea. "Oh Porter, is it really you?"

"As real as can be, and no worse for the wear," he said.

She rose, brushing her peek-a-boo bangs out of her face and ran over to embrace him. "It's so good to see you again; I can't believe how long it's been!"

"A year, like always," he said.

They seemed to know each other pretty well. I wondered if she was his granddaughter, or a niece. He leaned over and kissed her full on the lips, and she wrapped her arms around him. Geez, never mind. He had to be in his seventies. If she was his girlfriend, he was doing awfully well.

When they parted, Porter turned her around. "I want to introduce you to somebody," he said. "Peggy, this is, um…."

"You can call me Scott," I said.

She was about to comment, probably wondering how we knew each other, but the bartender came back with the scotches. Peggy ordered a sidecar and we took seats at the table.

"You picked a hell of a night to show up again, Porter," she said. "Joey's got something hot on the stove and it's going down tonight."

"Yeah, I heard about it," Porter said, giving me a wink. "That's why I'm here. I have a hunch what Joey's cooking is about to boil over, and I'm here to help him simmer it down."

"You heard about it?" Peggy arched her eyebrows and blinked with those long lashes.

"Doll, just because I ain't been around doesn't mean I don't have ears."

She put her hand on his arm. "Well, I'm sure glad you're here. Will it work?"

"It will this time." Porter drained his drink and stood. "I got some business to attend to. You mind showing Scott here around? Maybe introduce him to some of the kids." He disappeared into the crowd.

"So what's your story?" Peggy said to me. God, those green eyes.

"I'm from out of town. You and Porter known each other a while?"

"It seems like forever. I ain't dizzy with him, though, if that's what you're thinking."

I grinned. "You really have the lingo down, don't you? Is this like a throwback party or something?"

Peggy regarded me with an odd look. Just then, the guitarist on stage laid down a smooth jazzy crescendo of notes and Peggy's eyes widened. "This is my favorite song. You ain't a dead hoofer, are you?"

It took me a second. "Oh! I can dance to it if you want."

She was already up on her feet. "Lead the way."

I took her hand and brought her out to the dance floor and in seconds Peggy and I were face to face, dancing close. I thanked

God for those ballroom dancing lessons a girlfriend had made me take back in college. A little rough at first, but the steps to the waltz came back to me as the song went on.

"What's the name of this song, anyway?" I asked.

Peggy gazed up at me in disbelief. "When you say you're from out of town, you must mean the Yukon. You don't know *My Romance?*"

"I guess I am a little out of touch." We didn't speak then, just danced, the lush horns and strings of the ballad complementing the warmth of her slender body and her soft hands against mine. Maybe it was the scotch going to my head, but there was something about her—her perfume, her clothes, the little jokes, a kind of elegance I'd hardly ever seen in a woman. I almost had to laugh, because it occurred to me who she reminded me of: my grandmother, before she died.

"You're a different kind of guy," Peggy said, smiling up at me from under those red curls. The song ended, and we stood for a moment holding each other under the chandelier. Porter's intruding voice brought us back to reality.

"Sorry to break in like this, kids." He held a homburg under his arm. "I got it all set up. Come on outside so we can discuss this where we won't be overhead."

I took one last look at the dance floor, where couples swung each other around as the band started up a faster number with blaring trumpets and saxes. Porter pulled us through a hallway behind the bar and out the back door and we were right on the beach, crashing waves and mild night air, the brass section still blowing a hot tune faintly from the ballroom. Porter and Peggy walked ahead and spoke to each other in low tones. I didn't pay too much attention, content to follow and soak in the mellow atmosphere.

We strolled out almost to the surf and Porter put a hand on each of our shoulders. "Okay, you kids listen carefully if you don't want to end up in a Chicago overcoat."

"A what?" I said.

Porter laughed. "I forget about you. A coffin, Scott. Listen to me if you don't want to end up plugged."

I wondered if he was joking. "What are you talking about? You didn't say anything about that upstairs! What are you mixed up in?"

"Don't get jumpy on me now, Scott." His grip on my shoulder tightened. "If you two follow my instructions, there's a pot of gold waiting for you at the end of the rainbow."

"A pot of gold?" I pushed him away. "What does that mean?"

"Exactly what I said. And we'll cut you in."

I hesitated. I saw now why he'd brought me down here. He needed me for some kind of scheme. Still, Steph and I could definitely use the money…but at the risk of being shot? I liked a good bet, but this one sounded lousy. "Forget it. I'm not interested, and I should've gone to bed hours ago."

I spun around and headed back to the ballroom. A quick walk back to the hotel and I might still get in six hours of sleep before I had to get up.

Peggy came running up beside me on the sand, her hand taking mine. "Stop, Scott, okay?" Those sea green eyes peered up at me, begging. "Scott, please. Porter knows what he's talking about. We need your help." She traced a finger along my arm. "*I* need your help."

Any lingering thoughts of Stephanie fell out of my mind, as well as apparently any bit of common sense, because I did stop.

"*You* do?" I said.

She nodded, making her curls bounce, and I glanced up at Porter again. Slowly, I went back. To say it was against my better judgment is an understatement, but some part of me was telling my better judgment to go get stuffed.

Porter went on like there hadn't been an interruption. "Okay, Scott. Here's the plan: we're going to meet over at the marina in exactly thirty minutes. Peggy knows where the boat is. I've got one last thing I have to do. And Scott"—he pointed a finger at me—"if there's any trouble, let Peggy do the talking. Don't breathe a word."

"What kind of trouble?" I asked.

"The marina. Thirty minutes."

Peggy and I walked hand in hand along Coast Boulevard. An old-time auto passed us by. Black, sleek styling, white-rimmed tires. Owner kept it in pristine shape. "Fancy car. Lot of money around here."

"It's a Ford Model 48," Peggy said.

"Ha! You sure know your cars. You an aficionado?"

"Oh, that's a pretty common one," Peggy said.

I raised an eyebrow but didn't remark on that. We passed by a building with a little brick alcove and I pulled her into it. "A quick kiss, for good luck." She didn't object.

It was dark in the alcove, not quite private if somebody walked right by, but close enough. I drew Peggy close and put my mouth on hers, and she kissed me right back. Her dress was slashed to the waist at the back and my fingers ran up and down her spine while my other hand held her tight. She trembled against me and I breathed in fiercely. My hands were already exploring ways to get that dress out of the way when I felt something cold and hard in the small of my back. Didn't feel like something Peggy was doing, unless she hadn't told me about her metal thumb.

"All right, put 'em up where I can see 'em. Good. Now turn around slowly."

I did as the voice said, and found myself inches from one ugly mug, slicked back hair and scarred cheeks, an offset nose and a cloudy eye. The .38 Super he poked into my chest was a lot prettier, but just as mean. His breath reeked of cheap wine.

"Hey, now," I said. It was amazing how fast the blood had evacuated my lower body and started pounding in my head. "I don't know what the problem is, but let's talk about it first."

"Shaddup." He nodded at Peggy. "You. Out in the street where I can see you. That's it. Under the streetlight. Should be a familiar place to you." He snorted and his lips parted at his little witticism. I've seen warmer smiles on reptiles. He turned his attention back to me. "I don't recognize you. You ain't from around here."

"I'm from out of town."

"Where." Not a question, a command.

"I live in Fairfax, Virginia."

"Never heard of it."

"It's outside Washington, D.C."

Ugly Mug drew back at that. "D.C., huh? So you're a fed." He poked the gun in my chest again, hard enough to bruise. "I oughta off you right now."

I could hear words coming out of my mouth and I knew how unconvincing they must sound but I couldn't stop myself from talking anyway. "I'm not a fed, I'm really not. I just met an old guy at the bar, and—"

"Don't be stupid, Carmelo," Peggy said. "Sure you can kill him. But you know how much heat you'll bring down on yourself if you do that? You think the feds are gonna let something like that slide?"

Carmelo cocked his head and took a step back. "Yeah, okay. So what's the story, Peg? You're hanging out with the law now? What are you, a stool pigeon?"

"No, I'm still with Porter," she said. "But he's got a different kind of game going."

Carmelo had backed into the street and kept going. "Looks like it. You better hope he knows how to play."

"Oh, we're rolling with loaded dice this time." Peggy snapped her fingers and Carmelo turned and ran. He disappeared around a corner. "I don't suppose we can start up again where we left off?"

She gave me a grin, but I wasn't in the mood for that. "Why don't you start explaining what the hell's going on here?"

"Anything," she said. "What do you want to know?"

"I want to know what's going on!" I knew my face was reddening. "I've been led around, almost shot, and everyone's acting like it's an old movie! Is this some kind of reality show or game or something?"

"It's no game." Peggy sighed. "Porter and I cut a deal that's gonna make us rich. But it's tricky. He has to come back to my time to make it work."

"Your time? What does that mean?"

"Things are different for Porter now. He comes back, and he's older. But he knows what to do 'cause he's lived through it before."

"So you're not going to give me a straight answer."

"No, I really am."

I grabbed her by the wrists. "Then do it. Start talking."

Her eyes were wide. "Scott, I'm trying to tell you. When do you think it is? I mean, which year?"

"What are you talking about?" Panic welled up in my stomach and I tightened my grip. "You're still messing with me."

"Scott!" she cried out in pain. "It's 1937! That's the year we're in!"

Up the street a man was walking by, wearing a fedora pulled down low and a newspaper folded under his arm. I pushed Peggy away and chased after him. "Excuse me, sorry to bother you, sir."

The man wore a double-breasted gray suit. He glanced up. "I ain't got any spare change, mac."

"No, I don't want that. Can you just tell me the date?"

"April third." He turned to go.

"No, which year?" I asked.

He gave me a contemptuous look. "You outta lay off the sauce, you know that?"

"Can you just tell me the year? Please?"

"If you're serious, it's 1937."

Okay. All right. But I wasn't fully convinced. Not yet. "What was the Padres score today?"

"The who? Buddy, you're completely bats."

"How about the Dodgers?"

He shook his head. "I don't know. I don't follow Brooklyn."

"Do you mind if I take a look at your paper?"

"You know what?" he said, handing it to me. "You keep it. Just leave me alone, alright?" He strode off muttering.

I took it and unfolded it. *Los Angeles Examiner. April 3rd, 1937. British enact Government of India Act. Nazi legion in Spain bombs Republicans in Jaén, dozens dead. First social security checks mailed: Feds expect 20 million recipients by end of year.*

I raised my head from the front page, feeling dazed. So it really was true.

The marina lay in an area the sign called *La Jolla Cove,* where a big rocky spit of land arced out into the sea. Our footsteps echoed against the wooden planks of the dock while waves gently lapped below.

"It's Pier 6, Slip 144," Peggy said. The half-moon provided enough light to walk along the dock but not enough to read the signs unless we put our faces right up to them. About halfway down Pier 6 we found our set of boat slips and I nearly tripped over some bulk blocking the ramp.

I caught myself with a heavy step right on the edge, just short of falling off into the water. "What the hell was that?"

Peggy stopped a few paces behind me. I leaned over to inspect the dark bundle, poking at it with a finger. Cloth, warm and wet. I pushed it over and it spread out into a body. "Oh my God," Peggy said. "Is he dead?"

I pushed myself back up to a standing position. "Well, I don't think he's going to join us for dancing later."

We both froze then. The sound of footsteps reverberated across the dock. A figure swung a flashlight and slowly walked down. Peggy and I didn't say a thing, barely breathed, didn't run because there was nowhere to go where the figure wouldn't be able to see us. It stopped at the end of our pier, held the flashlight up to read the sign. I frantically tried to think. Peggy and I could probably make it down the ramp and into one of the boats, but what then? Probably better just to confront this guy. Maybe he'd back off like Carmelo. I tightened my hands into fists.

The figure strode heavily down the pier and stopped at the top of the ramp. I tensed my body, ready to leap at him.

"How're you kids doing?" It was Porter's voice.

We breathed out. Peggy pointed at him accusingly. "God, you almost scared us half to death."

"Sorry about that. Let's keep the volume down though, okay?"

"Sure," Peggy said in a low tone. "Get that flashlight over here and help us see who this poor sap is."

Porter swung his flashlight on the body's face. Peggy let out a little cry. "It's Joey!"

Porter muttered something that sounded to me like, "This is my least favorite part." He nodded at me. "How you holding up, kid?"

"Okay, I guess."

"You know what the deal is now?"

"I know what year it is, if that's what you're asking."

"Good." Porter leaned over and grabbed one of Joey's arms. "Come over and help me. We gotta push him off into the drink."

"What? You can't!" Peggy said.

"Shhh. Low voices." Porter looked up at her. "We've got to. He's gone, Peggy. His body is blocking our way, and if somebody finds him, there's gonna be a lot of questions we're not ready to answer."

I crossed my arms. "That's it, Porter. I'm not going any farther until I get an explanation. Dead bodies, guns, and how the hell you got me back fifty years before I was born."

Porter sighed. "Scott, you deserve an explanation, and I intend to give you one as soon as I can. But there is a safe on a boat that holds three million dollars in gold coins, and the men who own it will not hesitate to fill us with holes if they catch us here. I've arranged things so we have enough time, but our window is minutes. There's one thing only that's important right now: Will you or will you not help Peggy and me get this done?"

Three million dollars. I thought about those bills piling up at home and those midnight calls. Even a fraction of three million dollars would pay off everything we owed. And maybe get Steph off my case and back on my side.

"This man's already dead, Scott. But the money's still here. You can go back to the ballroom and go up those stairs to your regular life. Or you can change it. Are you in or out?"

I wavered. Peggy. The money. I wasn't real sure what was going on, but why not take a chance? I was obviously not making it to the morning session of the conference anyway. I took a deep breath and placed my wager.

"Fine. Let's do it."

Porter nodded and we each grabbed an arm and heaved the body over the side, followed by a heavy splash. No backing out now.

"Great. Let's find that boat. There's a lot of cabbage at stake here."

Slip 144 turned out to hold a large cabin cruiser, all burnished wood and brass fixtures. If nothing else, I'd certainly arrived in a classy-looking era. Cars, boats, clothes, everything seemed calculated to reflect a certain sophisticated style in life. Was my own time really an advance over this?

Porter and I stepped on board. "So what are we up to here?" I asked.

"There's a safe on board this boat and it holds a fortune," Porter said. "Peggy, you stand right here and whistle if anybody comes."

"Got it," she said.

We descended to a galley and Porter shone his flashlight around. "It's about two feet high, foot-and-a-half deep."

I opened up all the cabinets but found only regular dishes and glassware and pots. "Don't think it's here," I said.

We pressed on into the sleeping berth. "There—under the bunk."

I lifted up the dust ruffle and sure enough, a large safe was hidden underneath. With some effort we pulled it out. "So we open it?" I asked.

Porter laughed. "Sorry, no. We have to work for this one. We've got to carry it."

"Carry it? How far?"

"All the way back to the ballroom, kid."

Porter nodded and we hoisted that monster up. Good God it was heavy. Somehow we got that safe off the boat and staggered onto the pier. "Do we have time to rest a minute?" I asked between heaving breaths.

"Set it down," Porter said. "Sixty seconds, that's it." He pulled out a pocket watch to make sure.

"What do you want me to do?" Peggy asked.

"Go up ahead," Porter said. "If anybody sees us, or asks any questions, change the subject. Or distract them. Whatever you have to do."

When the minute was over we raised it up again and this time made it to the base of the pier. Sweat dripped off me and Porter didn't look in any better shape. He pulled a handkerchief out with one hand and soaked up the perspiration across his forehead. "Can't stop now," he said. "Been waiting too many years for this."

"Is this why you needed me here?" I asked. "To work me like a mule?"

He grinned. "We couldn't do this without you."

"But why didn't you bring bags for this? The safe probably adds two hundred pounds to what we're carrying."

Porter laughed. "Tried it before. That's how you get caught. People see you carrying bags down the street, you must be a thief. They see you carrying a safe, they figure you're doing what you're supposed to be, or you wouldn't be doing it out in the open. Crazy, isn't it?"

"Peggy said something about this not being your first time."

"Oh, no, not my first time doing this by a long shot." His face turned sober. "I want you to know something, Scott. I tried to save Joey for twenty years. I never could do it. But just because he's gone doesn't mean the money ain't here. And eventually, I figured out I could pull somebody through with me."

I wanted to ask more, but it was time to lift again. And so it went, until we'd covered the blocks to the ballroom. We stopped outside a locked door behind the building. The party must have been over because the music had stopped.

Our clothes were sweat-drenched. Peggy appeared from somewhere and handed each of us a Coke, heavy green glass bottles with grooves down the side. I drank mine down without stopping. Couldn't do anything about our sweat-sogged duds but that sure took care of the thirst.

Porter gestured towards the door. "Okay, Peggy, do your thing."

She pulled out a penknife and slid it into the lock, probing in and out a few times until the door creaked open.

"Good girl." He handed her the flashlight so she could illuminate our way inside. And for the last time, Porter and I lifted the safe and carried it down half a dozen steps into a utility room. We squeezed our way behind the boiler into a short corridor, at the end another small wooden door. Peggy jimmied this one too revealing a long, narrow room, complete with bar and barstools. A layer of dust suggested it hadn't been used in a while.

"Used to be a speakeasy," Porter said. He put his arm around Peggy's waist. "Where I met this dish, actually."

"Oh, Porter, cut out the smooth talk. Let's open it up." She shined the flashlight on the safe.

"Give me a moment to catch my breath, dollface." He pulled out a cigarette and offered me one. I shook my head. He lit his and took a deep drag.

"How about you fill me in what this is all about?" I said.

"Sure, we got time now. Nobody's going to find us down here." Porter blew out a cloud of smoke. "What do you know about the Great Depression, Scott?"

I shook my head. "What is this? A history lesson?"

"A lot more than that," Porter said. "But you have heard of the Depression, right?"

"Yeah. I graduated from high school and everything."

"Okay, good." Porter's cigarette glowed in the darkness. "How about Executive Order 6102? You ever heard of that?"

"Never."

"It was President Roosevelt's baby. You see, he got it in his head that people were hoarding gold, and that was holding up the economic recovery. So Executive Order 6102 authorized the government to seize all privately held gold." He took another deep puff.

"Yeah, go on," I said.

"So anybody with gold had to turn it in, thirty-five dollars a troy ounce. It was a fair price. But it could be a real problem."

"Why's that? Who cares if you're holding gold or cash?"

"Well, say you had a lot of gold and you didn't really want to explain how it'd come into your possession."

"You mean, like from a crime or something."

"Something like that," Porter said. The smoke from the cigarette curled around his homburg and drifted away into the darkness. "Of course, one option might be to take your illegal gold and head to another country."

"For instance, on a boat," I said. "Maybe even in La Jolla Cove."

"Hey, you're savvy," Porter said. "I knew I picked you for a reason."

"But all that can't be true. What about jewelry? Peggy's got gold earrings in right now."

Peggy laughed. "Oh, these don't count. What would Uncle Sam want with something this tiny?"

"She's right," Porter said. "Small amounts are exempt for jewelry, family heirlooms, that sort of thing. But large amounts have to be turned in. The U.S. Treasury makes damn sure of that."

"But what are you going to do with the gold?" I asked. "You can't explain where you got it any more than the people we're taking it from."

"Ah, but I don't need to. You see, after 1974, the gold trade became legal again. And Peggy and I will know exactly where to come back and get it."

"You're going to wait almost forty years to get rich?"

"I've waited longer than that now. Tonight's the night I finally change history."

I stared at Porter. Couldn't quite make out his features in the dark. But something had just occurred to me. I would've guessed earlier he was a pretty robust seventy-two, seventy-four. But that couldn't be right. Back in my time, he had to be pushing a hundred, maybe more. "How old are you anyway?" I asked him.

"Old enough that if it doesn't work this time, I won't get another chance," he said. He took a last drag and tossed the cigarette away. He fished a slip of paper from out of his pocket. "All right, enough talk. Shine the light over here, would ya doll?"

Peggy did and Porter got down on his knees and slowly spun the dial with the numbers on the paper—left, right, left. A barely audible click and the door swung out. Peggy aimed the light inside and gasped. Hundreds of gold coins glowed dull yellow under the narrow flashlight beam.

"Take a good look, kids," Porter said. "You'll probably never see three thousand troy ounces of gold again." He held out his hand and I helped him to his feet.

Peggy put her arms around him and kissed him on the mouth. "We did it! We finally did it, after all these years."

"Eighty of 'em, exactly," Porter said. He stopped suddenly, and whispered. "Did you hear something?"

"You're getting paranoid, baby," Peggy said. "Don't worry. We're set now."

But there were definitely voices coming from up above. Porter kicked the safe door closed and leaned over to spin the dial off. Without a word we hurried past the boiler, up the stairs, stopping right inside the utility room door. Porter cracked it a couple inches and nodded at Peggy. She peered through the slit.

"I think we're clear," she murmured.

Porter pushed the door out just far enough for us to shove our way through and slammed it back in place as four men in dark suits came around the corner.

One of the men lifted his coat to show a badge he wore on the inside. "Don't move! US Treasury!"

"Good evening," Porter said. "Can we help you fellas with something?"

The T-man stepped close. "What are you three doing out here?"

"Just getting some air," Porter said. Trickles of sweat ran down his face.

"You been working?" the agent said. His eyes darted left and right, suspicious.

"Dancing. Hot as hell in that ballroom. That's why we stepped out here."

"Hmm." T-Man sniffed. "You seen anything?"

"Not sure what you mean," Porter said.

T-Man looked us up and down. "I think you're hiding something."

Another dark suit ran around the corner. "Sir, after we impounded the boat, we caught several men fleeing over on Prospect Street."

Our T-Man turned to face him. "Okay, good. Put 'em in the cars. I'll be there in a minute."

I took a hard look at Porter. His face was pale, his eyes wide. I could tell he was shaken, for the first time all evening. He'd had everything all planned out up until now. It occurred to me he'd tried to get the gold for eighty years and this was as far as he'd ever gotten, and now he was going to lose again one last time. Well, he'd brought me into the game, and I wasn't going to let my partner down, not to mention my share of the payoff. Time to double down.

T-Man still had his back turned. I tapped Porter on the shoulder and gestured for him to lean over. I spoke right into his ear in a low tone. "While I distract him, you take Peggy and run. Don't stop for anything."

T-Man whirled around. "What'd you say to him?"

I stepped forward. "I have something I want to discuss with you guys." Porter and Peggy took off behind me.

"Hey, stop them!" T-Man cried out. All four of his men ran after them.

Before T-Man could collect himself I punched him hard, catching him on a cheekbone. He wheeled backwards and I sprinted in the other direction. Around the corner, through the back door, past the bar. Footsteps behind me. The dance floor was abandoned, except for a clump of more dark suits standing around a body on the floor. I slammed open the door to the stairwell and rushed up, hoping Porter and Peggy were already through.

I stopped mid-way up when I heard gunshots.

Two of them.

I gulped in a dry throat. I had a good idea who those shots were for. Now there was shouting at the bottom of the stairs. I took the remaining steps by twos and pushed my way through the door at the top.

And came crashing back into the bar with the ocean breeze. All the customers were gone and Jimmy was wiping down the bar with a rag.

"I'm sorry, it's past closing time," he called out.

"Sorry," I said, pausing to catch my breath. "Did somebody pass through here just now?"

"Nobody," he said. "What were you doing in the closet?"

"I was just down in the ballroom."

"The ballroom?" Jimmy tossed his rag behind the bar and gave me a funny look. "What do you mean?"

"Downstairs," I said. "I went down there with that old guy, Porter."

"Oh, Mr. O'Brien," he said. "That explains it."

I shook my head. This conversation wasn't making a lot of sense. Which was saying a lot, after the other events of the evening.

"The La Jolla Ballroom burned down in 1960, sir," Jimmy said.

"Nonsense, I was just down there."

"Go open that door you just came through," he said.

When I opened it a broom fell out. I blinked, tried to comprehend. It was a closet, just a few buckets and mops and cleaning supplies. My eyes were a little bleary, but surely I hadn't had that much to drink. I went in, trying to find the way back down the stairs, but the walls were all solid enough. I backed out.

"I don't understand it," I said. "Isn't that where I just came out?"

"Sure it is," Jimmy said. "Mr. O'Brien is one of our best customers. He's a real special one. Been coming here since the beginning."

"I gotta get back to the hotel," I mumbled, confused and more than a little irritated. I headed towards the door of the bar. The front door. "This leads outside, right?" I said, only half sarcastically.

"Yes, sir."

I'd only gone a few steps when I heard somebody beside me. I turned around. It was Jimmy.

"Sir, Mr. O'Brien left this for you," he said, holding his hand out. An envelope.

I took it and examined it. Plain white, my name in cursive across the front.

"Thanks," I said.

Back in my hotel room, I opened it up. Inside was a slip of paper which I unfolded. On it was written the combination.

I slept through both sessions of the conference that day and decided to pay the bar another visit. Jimmy was there again. "Another Oban, sir?"

"Sure, why not?" He poured me the drink. "You said last night the ballroom burned down in 1960. Are you positive that's what happened?"

Jimmy pulled out a cloth and wiped a water stain on the counter. "Well, it's not like I was there at the time. But that's what the sign says."

"The sign?"

"The historical marker. It's out by the street. Claims everything burned down to the bricks, but they saved the façade for the current building."

Down to the bricks. That meant there was still a chance, then. I downed my drink and threw a twenty on the counter.

At the bottom of the building I found a metal utility door, closed with a rusty old padlock. Could really use Peggy now. I found a cinderblock nearby instead. Glanced to each side. Nobody around. A couple hits sheared the lock right off. Inside I pulled out my phone for the glow. Steps. Ancient boiler. Squeezed by it, and down the corridor. And then nothing. Just bricked up at the end.

I sat on the floor and hugged my knees. What the hell to do now? I imagined Porter and Peggy back with the T-men, lying on the ground with their lives leaking out. Had they died right there? Or lived on? Then again, if Porter hadn't lived, how had I met him decades later, looking thirty years younger than he had any right to?

Too many questions, no way to answer them, and this stupid wall in the way. I brushed my hand across the surface and some of the mortar crumbled off. Huh.

I rose and gave the bricks a test kick. More mortar crumbled. This might work. I turned and put all my power into a rear kick with the heel of my shoe, and another, and another. I felt something give way. Another kick, and bricks tumbled. Another, and the opening grew. Soon I had enough room to crawl through.

On the other side I brushed myself off and raised the phone. The barstools, the dust. And there was the safe, unmoved for eighty years. And something else, on the floor. I bent over and picked it up. A penknife.

Back at the hotel I took a hot shower. I tried to puzzle things out. Porter had come back every year for eighty years, trying to find a solution. But by the end, he must have known he'd never get to enjoy the money. Was it just the principle of the thing, to finish what he'd started long before?

I got out and toweled off. Something glinted on the table under the lamp. The penknife. Ivory handle, curved to fit the palm. I opened the blade. And then I knew. That was why he'd done it: for Peggy. Beautiful, and ready for action when you needed her. For a dame like that, it would be worth it, even if she wasn't dizzy with you.

Stephanie and I walked in the bar. The night was as mild and amiable as they always are in La Jolla. Jimmy was behind the counter.

"Say, it's been a while since I've seen you," he said. "What'll it be?"

"An Oban," I said. "And for her, a sidecar."

Stephanie gave me a look. "A sidecar? I think you're mixing me up with my grandmother. I'll take a Glenfiddich with water."

"Coming right up," Jimmy said. "So how long's it been since we saw you last?"

"Exactly one year," I said. "Have you seen Porter around?"

"Oh, I haven't seen Mr. O'Brien in quite a while. Maybe not since… well, since the last time you were here."

Steph and I finished our drinks. I took her by the arm and led her to the broom closet. I opened it. The sound of horns came up from somewhere behind the line of mops.

"You ready to dance?" I asked.

"Are you sure it's through here?"

"Absolutely."

"Well, don't you think you should pay the man?" Steph nodded at Jimmy.

"Oh, right." I took a gold coin out of my pocket and flipped it in the air. "Call it."

"You're silly," she giggled, and reached over to straighten my bowtie. "Tails."

If her eyes were any browner they'd have been a cup of coffee, if her lips were any redder they'd have been cherry pie. I gave her a quick kiss and slapped the coin on the counter.

"Hey, Jimmy," I sang out. "Tonight I've got a date with the most beautiful woman in the world."

"Very good, sir," he said, and I pulled Stephanie through the broom closet and down the stairs. We had to hurry. The band was starting up *My Romance.*

THE METROPOLITAN

Sometimes my anxieties come out in my dreams. For whatever reason, frequent themes of such dreams include being trapped in an elevator and having to walk down aisles in a pet store filled with ghastly, oversized insects or aquariums of horrible, mutated fish. At the time I wrote this, I was having a tough time at work and two of these anxiety dreams took place within a week of each other. Once I shook off my initial middle-of-the-night revulsion, I found the dreams so intriguing I wondered if I could incorporate them in a story. The result is perhaps not the most coherent thing I've ever written, but I rather like the effect. Perhaps you will too.

This one has never appeared in print before. Those of you who don't like scary stories may want to skip it.

"Hello, welcome to the Metropolitan," the clerk at the front desk said.

Ben liked his mustache, pencil-thin and curled up at the ends in a rather impossible manner. "Yes, Ben Denton. I have a reservation."

"Of course, Mr. Denton." A tight smile spread across the man's lips. "We've been waiting for you." He poked a few times at the keyboard. "How was your drive in, sir?"

"Awful," Ben said. "Got caught in a rainstorm. A real squall. Took three hours to get here. But what a relief to arrive." He gazed around in wonder at the old-style opulence. Deep-piled burgundy carpets. Detailing in copper and carved teak. Porcelain ceilings. He'd stayed at some five-star hotels before but the magnificence here bordered on regal.

"Oh, how terrible," the front desk man said after a minute.

"I'm sorry?"

"About the rainstorm. How terrible."

"Oh, yes," Ben said. "Worst storm I've ever seen. Wasn't sure

I was even on the right road for a while there."

"Sounds exhausting." The clerk ripped a page off the printer and handed it to Ben.

"Been on my feet since three this morning. Flight from London. Delayed in JFK, and after I finally land in St. Louis, an hour in the rental car line. And the rain on top of all that."

"Here's your key," the front desk man said, his smile now more of a grin. "Room 910. The elevator is over there." He nodded to a corridor behind some potted palms. "The bell boy will be along in a minute if you'd like to leave your bags."

"No thanks," Ben said. He took the over-sized iron key. No keycards for this place. "I've only got these." He picked up his garment bag and his briefcase and treaded to the elevator door, each step sinking down into carpet like a layer cake. He depressed the single button, an old style pop-out with white lettering.

The floor indicator dial above the door flickered left from twenty-five, stopping every few floors for an extended wait. A musky odor, slightly sweet, drifted across the lobby. Ben glanced back at the front desk where the clerk still stood looking after him, his grin now a bit maniacal. Ben shook his head and returned his attention to the elevator. *Ding!*

He stepped on and pushed in the button for the ninth floor. The elevator ascended with agonizing slowness. Ben removed his glasses and rubbed his eyes. First a bottle of Perrier from the hotel fridge. And then nothing sounded more delightful than slipping off his Italian wingtips and sliding into the soft bristliness of high thread-count Egyptian cotton.

Ding! Ninth floor. Ben picked up his bags and strode into the hallway, but stopped on his heels when he saw the number plate on the first door. Room 701. Odd, he had gotten off at the ninth floor, hadn't he? He turned around just as the elevator door closed. *Dammit!*

Maybe the stairs instead. It was only two floors. He picked up his bags and hunted for the stairwell, but didn't see one after several doors. He peered down the hallway. Between the dim lighting and the dark mahogany paneling he wasn't quite sure he could even make out the far end, only a double row of doors to infinity. He sighed, and returned to the elevator, pushing in the button. This one stuck a little and he jammed his thumb.

The car arrived an indeterminate length of time later and Ben entered, still sucking on his thumbnail. He hit the button for the ninth floor and the door opened immediately. *Aha!* Smiling to himself, Ben pressed the button for the eleventh floor. *Must be a quirk of an old place like this.*

The elevator stopped at the tenth floor and a stooped old lady got on and pushed the "R" button at the bottom. The elevator started to descend.

"I'm sorry," Ben said. "But why is the elevator going down?"

The lady glared up at him from beneath a floppy straw hat. "I pushed the button," she said with a tone that indicated she was dealing with a real moron.

"Yes, I know, but I had already pushed the button for the eleventh floor."

"You new here?" she asked, pointing at his bags.

"Yes, it's my first stay."

"Here's my advice." She turned and faced the door. "Get out at the restaurant and get yourself a drink."

The door opened and she exited. A mood-lit bistro, all mirrors and polish, glimmered outside.

Well, as long as I'm here. Ben took his bags. He found a seat at a long, polished wood bar, glasswear hanging from the ceiling for what seemed like blocks. He glanced around at the tables. A number of patrons slept in the booths, their heads resting on folded arms or leaned against seatbacks, snoring noses sticking in the air.

A huge unshaven man with a giant gut hanging over worn bluejeans took the bar stool next to Ben. "Where you come in from?" he asked.

"Um, St. Louis," Ben said.

"St. Louee!" the man boomed. "Texan, myself."

"Uh huh," Ben said.

"Craziest thing." He sidled up so close Ben could smell body odor and stale cigarettes clinging to his red-checked shirt. "I was driving out here, and I had this cough, so I stopped at a gas station and picked up a bottle of cough syrup."

The man hacked wetly, as if to demonstrate. Ben hoped if he didn't say anything the story would end, but no luck.

"So I chugged about half the bottle, and took another sip every time I had a fit in the car. Before you know it, the damn bottle was empty!"

He paused expectantly. "So…" Ben said flatly. "What happened then."

"Well, I guess I must have passed out, or something. I was driving out west, you know, practically hit the New Mexico border. And it all gets kind of hazy, but when I came to it was the middle of the night, and I was in this little town. A village, really, with these little wooden buildings and all these Indians standing around, and there was a big bonfire in the middle of the road. And one of these Indians taps on the window so I rolled it down."

Ben glanced around, wondering if the bartender was even on duty.

"And he says to me, he says, 'Road closed, amigo. You got to turn around.' And I said to him, 'Buddy, I don't even know which road I'm on.'" Sweat ran down the Texan's chubby red face, as if telling the story was taxing him physically.

The bottles lined up against the mirrored back wall seemed dusty. *Has anyone ever actually gotten a drink at this place?*

"So I get out of my car and walk around it, and all these Indians are staring at me. And it was the middle of the night, and I'm trying to figure out why all these people are awake and standing around at that time. But I started gettin' the sense they didn't want no *gringo* around. A real menacing vibe, you know. So I get back in my car and hightail it out of there, and the sign on the highway says 'Mexico ahead.' And whoo-ee, I don't wanna end up there! So I take the first turn-off, and here was this place just a piece down the road. Crazy, right?" He pulled out a white handkerchief from his pants pocket and dabbed at his forehead.

"Great story," Ben said. *This man is deranged. New Mexico?*

"Well, thanks. How 'bout you, pardner? How'd you end up here?"

Ben sighed with irritation. "Do you have any idea how to get served?"

"Ha!" the Texan bellowed. "I ain't got a clue!"

Back in the lobby, the clerk grinned at him as Ben approached the front desk. Ben liked his mustache less this time, impressive as it still was.

"Is everything okay with your room, sir?"

"I wouldn't know," Ben said. "Just out of curiosity, is anybody working in the restaurant tonight?"

"Oh, yes," the clerk said. "We have a full staff on duty."

"Huh." Ben looked thoughtful. "Could I go ahead and get that bellboy to take my bags up?"

"Of course, sir. Just leave your bags over there." The clerk nodded to a niche next to the revolving door.

"I was hoping to go up with him," Ben said.

The clerk frowned, causing the tips of his mustache to bob. "I'm so sorry, he's helping another guest at the moment. If you'd like you could wait for him."

"No, thank you," Ben said. Out of the corner of his eye he noticed an elevator around the corner behind the check-in area. "I think I'll take that elevator this time."

"Oh, I'm sorry sir," said the clerk. "That's the service elevator. You don't want to take that."

Ben sighed. "I guess I'll carry my bags after all."

"Very good, sir."

Ben waited by the elevator door. This time the car arrived almost immediately. *Ding!* Ben got on and pushed in the button for the eleventh floor.

At the fifth floor the car stopped and a man in dirty jeans and a white v-neck undershirt got in. His finger reached for the "R" button.

"Wait!" Ben cried. The man froze, his finger an inch from the wall panel. "Would you mind letting me get off at my floor, first?"

The man grunted and pulled his hand back. The elevator reached the eleventh floor and Ben got off. At the first door, he checked the number plate: Room 1301.

"Bastard!" Ben swiveled around back to the elevator. *Ding!* The doors closed.

Ben slammed his bags down on the carpeted floor. *God my feet hurt so much. And that elevator's going to take goddamn ages getting back.* He meandered down the hall, stopping at a door on a whim. Room 1323. He listened at the door. No sound.

Ben took the iron key from his pocket and inserted it in the keyhole. He turned it slowly to the right.

Nothing.

He pulled it out the slightest bit and turned it again.

Nothing.

He slid it in about a quarter-inch and turned it, a click signaling the tumblers had fallen. He carefully turned the knob and pushed the door open.

No lights and the curtains were drawn. Air-conditioning blasted from the far end and the ice-cold air was a relief to Ben's overheated skin. He took a step into the room, and another. Something shifted in the bed, a body turning away from the intrusion of light.

Ben hesitated. He hadn't really expected the door to open, and had sort of suspected the hotel was mostly unoccupied, anyway. Apparently he was wrong on that count. *So tired. Why couldn't this room have been empty?*

The figure in the bed jerked up and turned towards him. A woman, sheets wrapped around her torso, raven black hair, her cheekbones shadowed in the stark rectangle of light. She looked him up and down. "So you're the one she sent this time."

Ben's forehead wrinkled in confusion. "Not me."

"Yes, you. She doesn't make mistakes like that."

"I'm sorry. I was looking for a place to lie down a few minutes. Until my room is ready."

She stretched leisurely and the sheet clung around the teardrops of her breasts. Her movement sent a hint of jasmine floating in the air currents. A faint smile teased the corners of her black lipsticked lips. "Are you open-minded?"

Am I open-minded? He stared at her hand, extended from under the blankets, her index finger tracing little circles on the sheet, and he imagined that was him, those little circles descending down, down. "I…I don't think so."

"Oh, that's too bad." The corners turned downwards. She patted the mattress. "You can still lie down, though, if you want to. It's so cold in here." She laid back, raven hair spreading across the pillow like a Japanese fan. "Take your shoes off and sit. We'll talk a little bit."

"There's been some kind of mistake," Ben said, backing out of the room.

"No, wait—"

He slammed the door behind him.

"You know, I think I will wait for the bell boy after all." Ben gripped the handles of his bags with such tightness his knuckles showed white.

"As you like, sir," the clerk said, without looking up from paperwork at the check-in desk.

"I do like." He sat on one of the blackwood chairs scattered around the lobby, dropping his bags to either side, sinking into its creamy cushiony seat, eyelids drooping. *Just rest here until the bellboy shows up.*

"Hey, hey mister!"

Ben's eyes snapped open. A middle-aged lady wearing a loud blouse and a cloud of perfume had taken the seat next to his. He checked the rest of the lobby. There were at least a dozen empty seats she could have taken instead.

"I didn't want you to fall asleep and get your bags stolen, yanno?"

"Mm, hmm?" Ben balanced between sleep and wakefulness and if this lady stopped talking he might be able to tip back over.

"You never know, right?" Ben didn't say anything so she went on, leaning over conspiratorially without lowering the tone of her voice. "Anybody could walk right through this lobby and pick up one of your bags and walk off with it, and you'd never find it again."

Her hot moist breath straight into his left ear had definitely pulled him away from that sweet edge. The vinegar tang of her perfume tinged by the chalkiness of her caked-on make-up. Ben straightened up and leaned away from her to escape the smell. "It doesn't seem like the kind of place likely to attract thieves."

The phone at the front desk rang.

"Oh, you're wrong about that," the lady said. "This is the kind of place they like best. It's swanky, that puts people at ease. All the carpets and furniture and the Mexican onyx and all that."

"The what?"

The phone kept ringing.

"The Mexican onyx. Yanno, the marble? The black marble with the veins in it." She gestured unnecessarily at one of the walls. "I don't like it, myself. Look at it too long, it seems like the veins are pulsing. Like the walls are alive or something. Yanno?"

It'd been at least nine rings and the telephone didn't stop.

"Why doesn't that clerk answer the phone? Probably hiding out in back somewhere." She mimed drinking from a bottle. "Yanno?"

Ben stood and hefted his bags. The clerk did seem to have disappeared.

"Hey? Where are you going?"

Ben didn't respond.

The woman leaned forward, sending another cloud of

perfume up Ben's nostrils. "I have an idea. If you wanted to catch a little shut-eye, I could watch your bags for you."

He strode to the hallway behind the check-in desk, almost tripping over a man curled up on the floor, in a red coat with brass buttons, his head resting on his hands. *The bellboy! He's been asleep here the whole goddamn time!*

"Where do you think you're going?" the lady called, a little frantically. She had risen and was walking towards him now.

He pressed the call button for the service elevator. The doors slid open. He smiled to himself. *Now I'm getting somewhere.* One last glance at the woman who had broken into a jog.

"You shouldn't do that! Don't get—"

The doors closed behind him. Oddly, there were no walls, just a wooden platform in a sort of service area, cinched around its edges with the pulley cables and fastened to the guide rail at the back. Pushbrooms and spare folding chairs were stacked in the cinderblocked area beyond. He dropped his bags. The only light filtered from the shaft above or through the crack where the doors didn't come together evenly. *How do I pick which floor?*

The elevator began to rise, as if it knew where to take him. *Maybe it goes straight to the kitchen? Or the laundry?* As he ascended, he could see the floors pass by. *Or maybe I'm supposed to just step off when I reach the right one? I guess they didn't worry too much about safety in the old days.*

The platform accelerated, gradually but steadily, until Ben felt distinctly uncomfortable with the speed. The spinning cable of the counterweight flashed in the shifting light. Past about the sixth or seventh floor the platform began to tilt to one side. He moved a step to the left, trying to even it out, but that only made it tilt to the other side instead. His garment bag slid slowly across the polished wood surface. He grabbed for it but the handle was wet from his sweaty hands and slipped away from the tips of his fingers. It glided right to the edge of the ever-more-slanted platform but Ben didn't dare reach for it now. He was too occupied trying to keep his balance, squatting with his arms spread, the platform swaying sickeningly under his wingtips. The garment bag teetered just a moment before dropping off into the gap, landing with a thump God knows where.

Quite suddenly the platform came to a halt at the top floor, the elevator machinery not far above Ben's head. He shifted his weight gingerly but it did not tilt further. There was a gap of about two feet between the platform and the floor and he jumped it, landing on his side with a thud but grateful for its solidity.

My briefcase! He looked back, wondering if he was brave enough to make the leap again. But without his body there to anchor against, the briefcase had also begun sliding and fell into the open air.

A rustling from somewhere in the dingy dim and Ben pushed himself up on one hand in an inch-thick layer of dust. The rustle, like papers brushing, drew closer and a long body slithered out of the darkness. Ben held his breath as the snake passed by within feet of him, its tongue flicking with audible clicks. For a moment it looked at him and opened its mouth slightly, revealing two rows of human teeth. But it did not stop, just brushed along, leaving a trail in the dust.

Ben exhaled and slowly rose to his feet. The space seemed endless, the weak light from the elevator shaft swallowed up, piles of junk jumbled about in twilit shadow. When he breathed in a sweet musk, strongly organic, filled his nose. In the distance, in a beam of light from somewhere above, sat a huge wooden armchair, almost a throne.

Ben approached it, walking gingerly. He felt somehow he might wake things he did not want to were he to make too much noise. Scores of little feet pattered rapidly away in the gloom as he moved. *Rats?* But they sounded heavier than rats.

The chair rested under a skylight, streaked and stained so the moonlight came down in spatters. The chair was large but nothing special, no cushions or inlays, might as well have been made out of plywood. But tempting.

So tired.

Ben sat in it and slumped back. The musk scent was even stronger here, like a fog. His arms gripped the armrests, his eyelids fluttered closed.

He woke with a jolt when he felt something crawl on him. His eyes widened and his lungs involuntarily drew in sharply.

A huge black beetle, as big as a baseball, crept up his right forearm. A pair of serrated pincers jittered off the creature's head, its black eyes rotated in their sockets. It hesitated a moment…smelling? Tasting? Waiting? Ben stayed as perfectly still as possible, slowing his breathing and hoping the single drop of sweat rolling down his temple did not drip.

A ticklish feeling climbed the fingers of his left hand, but he could not see what it was for his hand lay draped over the armrest and he did not dare raise it. His heartrate spiked as a millipede, fully half a foot long, came up over his wrist. Segments smoothly slid over each other and its antennae quivered as it crawled. He was torn between an urge to spring up and shake them off, or not to stir at all and hope they went away. He picked the second option. But they did not go away.

An itch formed on the back of his neck that he could not scratch. It spread up the side of his head and he realized it was not the random firing of a nerve-ending but another creature, multiple vibrating legs stretching from the nape to under his left earlobe. He swiveled his eyes as far in their sockets as they would go but he could not make it out. *Don't scream.*

A whisper in his ear, sibilant and harsh: "Good advice. My sisters are hungry and if you stir they will take you for prey."

It heard me!

"Quite clearly."

It…you can read my mind?

"I can hear every thought rattling around in your head like the screams of a fly in a web."

What do you want from me?

"You have traveled far to see me. But tell me, why did you

turn down my hospitality?"

I don't know what you mean.

"The gifts, you fool!" The legs tightened on his neck. On his right arm, the beetle's pincers closed and opened eagerly. "My servant offered you drink for you were thirsty, but you did not drink."

In the bar? No one was there to serve me.

"Serve you! You are not a master to be served. My servant told you to serve yourself."

Silence.

"And then my servant offered you love, and you turned her down. Did you not find her beauty pleasing?"

I…I did not think that was for me. And I was worn out.

"Ah, you were weary. Surely then, you should have taken up my servant's offer to watch your bags?"

I didn't want to let them go.

"And where are your bags now?"

Gone.

"I see. So you accepted nothing, and you lost the pitiful little you had. I find you detestably small, Ben Denton."

I'm so tired. All I want is to go to sleep.

"How I long for one who dares! For one who will take what I so freely give. But I am nothing if not merciful. I shall grant your desire."

Ben got off the elevator at the restaurant. The patrons still slept on their crossed arms. He probed a little at the itching twin-pitted sore on his back of his neck, wondering how it got there. His finger came away wet, but not bloody. He held his finger to his nose and breathed in the metallic cloying odor. *So tired. I could sleep for days.*

He found an empty booth and sprawled into it, relaxing his body in its enveloping cushion. He pushed his shoes off and let them drop to the floor. Almost involuntarily his head fell forward into his waiting crossed arms. All the muscles in his body relaxed. And just as he was drifting off, he was brought back to glaring wakefulness with a clap on his back.

"There you are, pardner! Where'd you get off to?"

STEADER

This one first appeared in the 2018 Writers of Chantilly anthology, Islands. *I remember when reading it out loud before the group, somebody mentioned that they wondered how I was able to write so well from a woman's point of view. I don't believe it's ever been an issue for me…writing from a woman's POV is no different or harder than writing any other character. You just have to put yourself in the character's place and see the world through their eyes, no matter their age, gender, race, education level, or whatever. Simply part of the writing process.*

1.

I would give my left ovary for a glass of pinot grigio," Medea said to the figure on the screen of her tablet. "I mean it, Treva. I could kill a man for a bottle of wine right now."

Treva laughed. "Don't go stir crazy on us now! We'll see you in two days. And we're stocked—all the wine you want to trade for."

"Oh, one more thing," Medea said. "I haven't been getting a full charge in my powerwall. I need to get somebody to look at it."

"Uh oh," Treva said. "Definitely don't want anything messing with your power. Any idea what the problem is?"

"I checked but didn't see anything obvious." Medea idly ran her thumb along a patch of sea salt flaked on the table. "Could be the inverter, maybe."

"Ask Henry to take a look at it," Treva said. "He takes care of all our equipment like that here."

"Great. Two days then. Looking forward to it."

"Us too, honey. It's been too long."

Medea closed the cover on the tablet and tossed it into the seat next to her. Out the window, the sun approached its highest point and curly white cirrus clouds wisped to the horizon. Medea smiled and rose, exiting the center living module and striding along the deck. Her steadcraft was a perfect circle, two hundred-forty feet across, and fully self-sustaining. Rows of corn bobbed gently in the constant sea breeze, and the vines of heirloom tomato plants hung heavy-laden from their metal cages.

She and Jason had thought about making their own wine, but the trellises required for the grapes would have been too tall—would have interfered with the gliding of the solar panels and the drip irrigation. Same with the apples and peaches she longed for. Trees would grow way too high, plus the roots would spread underneath the deck. It was amazing how much growth could be packed on such a small surface, but only with careful consideration of the space required for each addition. Well, maybe they'd have some fruit at Puerto Libre to trade for.

She stopped at the raised lip at the edge of the deck and leaned against the railing, staring out at the sea. Hecate appeared from somewhere, rubbed against Medea's legs, meowed, and leapt up to the top so she could better scratch his head. It never ceased to terrify her when he strolled along the rail, where one false step could plunge him into the brine, but he did not notice the danger. She petted him and slipped an arm under his body, lifting him away from the edge.

"Down you go! No need to feed the sharks today."

Nearly midday, time to adjust the solar panels. She climbed up and shifted them along the tracks on their framework, maneuvering them over the potatoes and carrots, where they would provide needed shade for these cool weather plants. She pressed a switch and tilted the panels to maximize their sun exposure. With the powerwall leaky, she wanted to soak up all the power she could get.

Morning chores done, and a half hour to lunch. Just enough time to catch some rays.

One thing you couldn't beat was the tanning.

Lying out on the sundeck above the living module, the hot sun spreading across her body like melting butter, temperature balanced by the perpetual breeze of the open ocean. She reveled in the solitude of being the only living soul for a hundred miles or more.

Not that she didn't get lonely sometimes. It hadn't always been that way. Before, Jason had been there, and the two of them had been enough. Working on the steadcraft in the morning—he could've fixed the powerwall in an hour, while she tended to the vegetables and herbs. Scrabble after dinner. Splitting a bottle of wine. Making love at night and—why not?—again the next morning.

She traced a finger around her earlobe, across her cheek, as he used to do with his flicking tongue. Lightly along her neck, her sternum, around the outer edge of her breast, the areola, down her stomach, across the shallow indention of the femoral triangle, her breathing quickening and excitement spreading from her inner thighs. Her foot pointed and she raised a knee slightly to allow the tips of her fingers—

She froze.

Medea felt something she had not felt in a long time. She almost laughed out loud to think it, it was so impossible. Here, in the one place it could not possibly happen.

She felt that someone was watching her.

Silly.

Still, the spooky sensation ended her tanning session. She rose and put a towel around her, shaking her head at herself. Oh, well. She needed to cut some mint from the herb garden for her lunch salad anyway. Maybe pluck some motherwort leaves to crush into a calming herbal tea.

Medea sipped her tea. A bit bitter for her taste, but Treva would have some lemons. She already felt the calm spread through her body, numbing the bizarreness of the tanning incident. She knew the source of that invasive feeling, of course. Obvious, once she reflected on it.

That fishing vessel she'd met four days ago. Hailed her on the radio, asked if she wanted to trade. Not so unusual to see another vessel on occasion, a little less so to interact, but not unheard of. A Korean-flagged boat with a mixed crew.

Steaders were known for providing substances illicit in much the rest of the world. Medea had made it plain she didn't have any of that. The smiling, bronze-faced Korean man, the captain, explained in surprisingly good English: "We have plenty tuna, no vegetables. Out here two more weeks. What you give for tuna?"

Hadn't seemed like a bad deal at the time. Get rid of her excess of cucumbers and squash. Throw in some eggs. Stock up her deep freezer with fish. Favorable terms of trade, too.

The Korean captain had showed concern that she was out on the high seas by herself. "You all alone out here?"

He'd given her an avuncular smile and his words had a friendly tone, but they reminded her of things past. She'd glanced around, suddenly aware she was the only woman, with a crew of perhaps a dozen men on the other side. She squashed a tendril of irrational fear and smiled back. "I like it that way."

He'd squinted at her steadcraft and back at her. "You handle that big thing by yourself?" She'd assured him she had been handling it by herself for a long time now.

Not much about the crew stuck her now, except for one man. Stayed off to the side, by himself. And no wonder, with burns covering much of his face. She hadn't so much seen him as *not* seen him, intentionally averting her eyes. But she had found her line of sight drifting towards him once or twice, his fleece stocking cap worn even in the tropical air, his fascinatingly marred features sagging molten folds across his cheeks as if he'd only just stepped out of the flames and his skin were still soft.

He'd sensed her interest and stared back. Hardness behind those eyes. An onion peeler of a gaze. Like he'd stripped her down of her clothes and her skin too.

She'd thought about him later, reviewed that wilting face in her mind: cheese in the toaster oven, a watch in a Dali painting. What kind of place could a man like that have in society? A tuna boat in the middle of the Pacific, that was the place.

She snapped her fingers. *Right, the tuna.* If she wanted a tuna steak for dinner, she'd better set it out to thaw. Actually, it was probably too late for today. She'd have to stick it in the fridge so it'd be ready tomorrow.

They had Jason by the arms, two of them. It was surprising how small they were, not big men at all. Short and acne-scarred and big-eared, grinning at their prize. A third one sauntered up and walloped Jason in his belly. A thump and an audible groan. All Medea could do was stare.

He glanced up at her, silently mouthing the words: "Go! Godammit, go!" And then a fourth one, the leader, had pulled out a butterfly knife and she cringed to see what happened next. The blood flowed from Jason's side, but she felt the heat against her chest, as if that blade had slid right between her own ribs.

Medea sat straight up in her bed, her hair a mess of sweat. Hecate leaped to the floor, miffed at the disturbance. She patted the sheets were he'd lain, the warm spot where he'd nestled against her side. Odd for him to sleep right next to her instead of his preferred spot at her feet. Still, that explained the one part of her nightmare, at least.

What's gotten into me?

And then it struck her. It was the first of August. The anniversary was only one day away. She'd pushed it out of her head, but she must have known subconsciously. She checked her watch: 5:00 AM. Well, she might as well get up and do the chores.

First thing was the chickens. Medea got a bowl of feed and spread it around the chicken coop, drawing the half dozen hens from wherever they unhurriedly pecked for worms and insects.

"Good morning, ladies. What do you have for me today?" She checked the coop and found three eggs. Fine – two for breakfast and one to refrigerate. Worrisome though. This was the third day in a row with low production. Normally she got five or six. "Lucy? Brigitte? Aren't you ladies feeling well?

Not a lot of seasteaders kept chickens—too messy. But Medea found they kept her company, and eggs provided a nice addition to fish. Their droppings were high in nitrogen, great for the tomato plants. Plus, a couple dozen fresh eggs were always a nice bonus to throw in if a bartering partner was balking at an exchange.

She stopped and plucked a couple ripe tomatoes to add to her omelette. One had a rotten hole in it. Hopefully they weren't infested. Fruitworms could spread to the corn and the okra. On a steadcraft, that would really play havoc with carefully planned menus and trade goods. She'd have to check later for eggs on the leaves.

She opened the refrigerator, searching for the peanut butter. Not in its usual place. *Did I finish the jar already?* Something else to trade with Treva for. She made a mental note to add it to her list.

A crash from outside, a flurry of squawks and clucks and feathers rustling. Medea dashed towards the coop, nearly tripping over Hecate sprinting in the opposite direction with tail outstretched. A roosting bar had fallen against the mesh wire floor. An ungodly racket, but not a huge problem. She could fix it later.

That damn cat. But it was strange. Hecate was well-fed, and he'd never been too concerned with the chickens before. *Good God, I'd better eat my breakfast before something else breaks.*

The ocean drank the red setting sun, sending bloody streaks across the waves from horizon to horizon. In the north, a hint of black mounted, lit from time to time by tendrils of lightning.

Medea checked the weather report again. The storm had come up from out of nowhere, but that could happen out here on a late summer afternoon in the warm waters of the mid-Pacific. If she wanted to make civilization by the morning, she'd have to power through it. Well, a little rain never hurt anyone.

In the kitchen she sliced lettuce, onions, cilantro, and tomatoes. Lemons would have been the perfect final touch, but still, she had enough for a salad with her fish. She expertly cut the tomatoes into quarters. One tomato was bad; black and mushy on one side. *Fruit worms.*

"That's it!" She marched out to the tomato plants. She had to find the eggs before this became a real problem. Only all the plants looked fine. Healthy, reddening tomatoes. Maybe in the morning she'd check again. She saw something on the ground out of the corner of her eye and leaned over. A brown seed.

She picked it up. Teardrop-shaped. An apple seed. But she didn't have any apples. Slowly, an idea seeped into her consciousness.

The tanning incident hadn't been just a feeling.

She was truly not alone.

Medea stood frozen for long moments, not daring to turn her head. But she did, finally. Nobody was there. She exhaled, realizing only then she'd been holding her breath.

She was being ridiculous. Nobody was on board. Where would they even hide? One of the sailors had gobbed the seed out when they'd brought the fish over and it'd landed on her deck. Or it was from long ago.

But…still. It could be. A stranger, unwelcome. On her floating island. It seemed almost impossible, but it wasn't, really. It was a bit smaller than average as steaders went, but there were numerous crannies, gaps behind equipment, even the honeycombed foam lining the hull.

She sniffed the air. Something was burning. The tuna steak. She dashed back to the galley.

Medea carved around the charred portion of the tuna. There was quite a bit salvageable, but she still wasn't hungry for it. She forced herself to eat, knowing she would need the energy this night. At the very least, she had to search every inch of the place. She picked up the dishes and brought them to the sink, washed them deliberately while she thought.

Let's say there is an intruder. Think it out. Would she confront him head-on? She would have to, at some point. Obviously, if he was there, he'd come on board from the fishing boat. Now he was hidden somewhere on the steadcraft, had been for days, watching her, eating her produce, staring at her lustfully while she tanned or slept.

Maybe she should have kept Jason's gun. The only thing they'd ever really argued about, and she'd traded it away months before. But she decided she was better off without it—after all, the intruder could have used it on her any time since he'd boarded.

And that was another matter. He'd had four days. Why hadn't he attacked her yet? Surely he wasn't just a stowaway. What was he waiting for?

She shook her head. *So juvenile, Medea.* She'd give the steadcraft a good once-over for her peace of mind, and go to bed.

And then the lights went out.

2.

Medea stood corpse-still, hands still immersed in soapy water. *Stay calm. It's a problem with the powerwall, that's all.* She'd been having issues with it. Something had gone wrong, a loose connection, a frayed wire.

But she knew that wasn't right. It was on purpose. *Think, Medea, think. Say there* is *an intruder on the ship. Why hasn't he done anything? And why the power drain? There has to be a reason.* A wine cork bobbed in the dishwater, spinning around in the bubbles.

Kind of like a mini-steadcraft. Maybe there was a little miniature Medea on the top of that cork, waiting for some bad guy cork to come along. Medea gasped. *That's it!*

She dried her hands, grabbed a pair of binoculars. As she climbed the metal ladder to the tanning deck, a few drops of rain splashed on her skin, the leading edge of the storm. Wind had picked up, too.

She put the binoculars to her eyes and scanned the ocean. There, due east, on the very edge of the horizon. A dingy catamaran. Fast though, the kind preferred by pirates. Appear out of nowhere, attack a cargo ship or a steadcraft, gone before help can arrive. That's what the intruder had been waiting on. He'd been signaling. Probably explained the powerwall drain too, powering some beacon or emitter. And now, once they'd established visual contact, cut the power.

How long did she have? From this vantage point, the distance to the horizon was eight miles. A catamaran like that should cover twice that distance in an hour, but the waves were choppy. Might be more like forty-five minutes. No time to waste, in any case.

Back in the dark living module, she didn't need light; she knew this place well. In the kitchen, she led her fingers across the countertop to the wooden knife block and selected the fish scaling knife with its comfortable grip and thick blade, whistle-sharp on its curved side and serrated on the other. *Just in case.*

Outside again, rain falling steadily now, fat drops collecting in her hair and sliding cold down her back. Down the spiral staircase into the powerwall room, the rubbery surface of the non-slip stairs compressing under her bare feet and one sweaty hand gripping the knife.

Red and green glowing and blinking dots came into view, and she stopped on the bottom stair to calm her breath. The blinking lights were a good sign.

It was completely quiet in the narrow room, without the

usual low hum from the equipment. Still, from what she could tell, the powerwall had simply been shut down rather than damaged in some way. All she had to do was press the main power switch and it should start up on its own. Other electronics on the boat might require restarting too, but she could figure that out later.

She ran her hands along the surface, searching for the indentation of the power switch. A creak from behind her. She stopped, slowly swiveled her head.

In the back corner a figure crouched, about five feet away, dark, hooded. He'd certainly noticed her. Neither moved for a long minute. A low rumble of thunder resonated outside, vibrating the boat to its core.

It was amazing how calm she felt, now that it was true. The figure leaped at her and she jabbed upwards with her knife hand, but the knife glided over leather and into free air and the figure was quick, catching her around the waist and knocking her to the floor. Her head and shoulder thudded painfully against the bricked batteries of the powerwall. He was on top of her and sour sweat and body odor filled her nostrils. The arms constricted around her, shoving her along the bumpy floor, roughly groping her back, her arms, her breasts, finding her throat and squeezing. Each individual finger dug in until she could feel tendons in her neck split.

No air and no thoughts, only pure panic. But somehow in her state she had held onto the knife and she jammed it into his side, drove it until the point punctured leather. Deeper then, into pulp and bouncing against bone. The figure reared back and spat curses in a foreign tongue. He pushed himself up and staggered up the stairs. She managed one look at his face as he fled in the dim light.

The right side was covered in burn scarring.

Medea gulped air for several breaths without sitting up. She put a hand to her face, to her neck. Tender, but nothing broken. Probably lots and lots of bruising later.

Her eyes blinked closed and she faded. For a moment, she screwed up her resolve and opened them, trying to will herself from passing out. Her eyes fluttered closed again and things went black.

That night again. She had heeded Jason's command, fled while she could, but to where? Their steadcraft was occupied so the only place she could go was the pirates' boat, sneaking up the gangplank, not that stealth was necessary as drunk as they all were. Nasty old catamaran greasy with diesel fumes. But they used kerosene for their personal use—cooking, most likely. She'd spread the contents of that fifty-gallon drum all across the deck, the personal quarters, the control room, against a backdrop of the men's inebriated laughter and her husband's screams and begging for his life in the black air.

She'd been patient, waiting for the pirates to return, sloshed and jolly with their evil, carrying away what they wanted as booty—bottles of wine, her jewelry, sonar, satellite radio equipment—and she'd slipped quietly overboard and back to her own vessel, but not before lighting a match.

It'd been positively beautiful as she'd engaged the engines and, with a jerk, pulled away from the orange-blue funeral pyre. She'd held Jason's lifeless body in her arms, its face so swollen and blued with bruising she couldn't recognize him. But the screams of burning men provided a measure of satisfaction, and she had gorged herself on them. Sound carries a long way on open water.

Medea came to and her eyes snapped open. Still slumped in the dim glow of the powerwall. Tired. Achy. She wanted to go back to sleep, but knew she couldn't. Had to find the intruder. But she suspected he was in worse shape than her, as that wound of his continued to bleed.

She grabbed the knife and forced herself to her feet, stumbled to the far end of the powerwall, initiated power up. It responded without any problems, though it would take several minutes for everything to come back online, at least what didn't need to be restarted manually. She found the magnetic penknife attached to the powerwall for occasions just such as this and slipped it in her pocket.

Medea tried to stand straight. Her knees staggered. She nearly fell, only barely catching the handrail of the stairs as a swirl of dizziness overtook her. Carefully she made her way up the stairs to the deck. Rain spit in the open door at the top and she closed it behind her. She was soaked almost as soon as she stepped out. Water spouted out of the sky, and it was nearly pitch black.

She had to get to the living module, boot up the guidance and steering computer. She stumbled around, nausea rumbling in her gut as she tried to stay on the paths, slipping repeatedly to the ground. It was taking much longer than it should—in her disorientation and the dark, she'd somehow lost her way. A flash of lightning gave a glimpse of the whirling sea, and she realized the dizziness was not her—it was the steadcraft. Of course, without power, there was no rudder control. They were spinning freely across the ocean.

Another lurch knocked her down again, where she came face to a face with a chicken sitting and miserably dripping right in the middle of the path.

"Oh, Lucy," Medea said. "What are doing out in this weather?" But her words were lost in the wind. She picked the soaking bird up, tucked it under her arm, baby steps to the henhouse. Another round of lightning and she saw the door had blown off the coop. And in the herb garden, lit briefly like a stadium, half the plants lay trampled to the dirt by bootprints.

Medea gritted her teeth. *That asshole.* At least she knew which direction he'd gone.

She stuck her head inside the coop. The hens were lined up along the top perch, nervously clucking. She gently placed Lucy among her sisters. Odd. Lucy was one of the more sensible ones.

Maybe she'd simply been caught by a gust of wind when the door blew off. Anyway, the henhouse was bolted to the deck, so they should all be safe enough. As safe as anything on a night like this. Medea was almost tempted to curl up in the relative dryness of the henhouse herself.

She ducked out and a hand grabbed her hair and pulled her down, forcing her face into cold mud. She slashed out ineffectually with the knife, but another hand had her now by her upper arm, yanked her back to her feet, and she got her first good look at the man: no taller than she, his black hair slicked back in the wetness, water running diagonally along the burn grooves on his cheek.

"Three years," he hissed in her ear, heavy accent pronouncing the three as 'tree.' "Three years I search for you. Three years I wait. My companions, dead. All dead. And me, six months in burn unit. After, my face. Hideous. But tonight, you know pain like me."

Pain? This was the man who'd crushed her motherwort. This was the man who'd helped kill her husband. And this was the man who had—

A squall cut her thought short, the boat listed wildly, and they tumbled together across the deck, through a patch of corn. Medea's stomach twisted as much from nausea as from seeing her hard-worked crops battered and flattened.

He lost his grip on her, but they were still entangled. She got to her feet first while he was on his knees. She swung at his face but he blocked her knife hand. More lightning illuminated the scene, and she saw something he didn't. He rose, she ducked, and a free swinging steel bar hit him in the back of the head and knocked him to the ground. Part of the irrigation and solar panel framework. Another damn thing that would have to be fixed in the morning, but she could hardly feel more grateful for it now.

But the man was not out yet. He crawled across the deck. She ran after and kicked at him; he grabbed her foot and she tripped. Another lurch, another sheet of rain, and she lost track of him.

No—there he was, he'd somehow found a hatch and heaved it open, disappearing inside. A little used compartment that led to the keel, used only for occasional repairs.

Aching, knife in one hand and penlight between teeth, Medea crawled through the foam lining honeycombed around the hull of the steadcraft. She had followed the intermittent drips of water and blood down here, to the true bowels of the ship. The passages provided room enough for movement on hands and knees and no more.

She halted to catch her breath and listen. Yes, up ahead, somewhere in the maze, the squeak of pressure against polyurethane. She popped the penknife back in her mouth and set off. She wasn't sure if she was on the hunt or prey heading straight into the trap, but she was eager to end this chase.

Left, left, straight for a while. She came to a pile of trash—eggshells (had he eaten them raw?), chocolate bar wrappers, an empty jar of peanut butter (aha!). And a plastic case, about two feet square. She opened it. It housed a mechanical device, face covered with knobs and switches, a spool of wire on the top. *The transmitter.* He must have used the wire to plug into the powerwall at night. *How many hours did he sit up on the deck with that while I was sleeping?*

She pushed all the junk aside and crawled onwards, around a vertical loop that flipped her on her back, requiring her to roll over, penlight beam flitting crazily across the white walls. A moist smear of blood across the white surface where he must have passed only moments before. She redoubled her pace now, right, left, and around the next corner she could hear his breathing, even heavier than hers, ragged and uneven. He must know she was there. Her knuckles showed white where she gripped the knife.

Moments. Minutes. The only sounds their panting, rhythmic, inhalations and exhalations phasing into and out of synchronization. It was impossible to tell how long. She flipped the light off. All is equal in the dark, right? She lunged around the corner.

Stabbing, knife hitting a boot and glancing off. She forced it again farther up, skidding off the foam wall, his rough hand sliding across her face until it slipped into her hair and pulled her on top of him, their breathing in synch again, faces inches apart. His hot breath was in her ear, his grotesque face touching her cheek, and her instrument finally finding purchase; a wet place she twisted with sickening glee. This close, that sour sweat smell again, it felt almost…intimate.

That night, three years ago, it flowed back to her. The pirate ship, somebody's bed chamber. He and the other pirates having their way with her, but he chiefly, his face not mortified then, but rough with whiskers, handsome maybe under different circumstances. Jason back on the steadcraft, tied up, helpless, she hoped she might buy his life with a good performance, so she acted like she loved it. Screaming with theatre, with ulterior motive, but hating every second and loathing them all, her revulsion all the greater because of her act. She had made her body respond, arched her back, meeting each thrust for every man, thinking that would satisfy them. And when it didn't, when they'd dragged her wrung out back to her own steadcraft and made her watch their fun with her husband, deep inside her a craving had grown for vengeance.

Her revenge that night, the consuming fire, had been enough for what they'd done to Jason, but not for what they'd done to her. And now here she had her chance to truly return the favor, to penetrate this man, to give to him what he had given to her. She ground the knife deeper. Did he appreciate it? Yes, he did, moaning as she rammed the knife as far as it would go and blood-streaked spittle bubbled out his lips. He jolted and his body relaxed under her.

The storm must have separated the steadcraft from the pirate ship. *Hopefully the bastards sank to the bottom of the ocean,* Medea thought as she steered the ship in the early morning sun. Rain had scrubbed the steadcraft, and the world, clean. Bushes laden with berries glistened, water collecting beneath them in fat drops and falling to the deck with little brilliant splashes. Newly brave chickens ventured forth for their morning feed. Hecate rubbed against her legs. And in the far distance, something glinted white.

It gradually came into view. Puerto Libre. An island, a whole community, of steaders, boats abutting or connected with planks or even elaborate pedestrian bridges, some growing crops, some with workshops or junkyards or trading posts or mini-foundries.

Medea coolly glided around the right side of the mass of steadcraft, smiling when the blue-and-white checkerboard pattern of her destination came into view. Treva's place—and there she was, brown hair in ringlets, arms folded and supporting her weight at the viewing deck. She spied Medea and gathered up her peasant skirt, running down to her main level in bare feet. Medea expertly pulled her magnetic latching gate to where it met Treva's and cut the propulsion.

Treva was waiting for her with open arms.

"Oh my God, girl, it's been too long!" She embraced Medea and then pushed her back to arms' length, eyeing her up and down. "Jesus, Medea, you look like shit."

"You remember what I said on the radio?" Medea asked. "About the wine?"

"Something about killing a man for a bottle of pinot grigio, I think?"

"Exactly," Medea said. "Go get the damn bottle."

FAVOR IN THY SIGHT

This is the first time this story has ever appeared in print. It's a retelling of Abraham's sacrifice of Isaac, from the Bible, a story I've always found somewhat disturbing. I think this was my attempt to make sense of that difficult Biblical account, though I'm not sure it helped.

You can't imagine how much my husband hated it when I found God. Please, please don't tell him what happened. I've had two miracles in my life, and I don't want to try to kill the second one, too.

Early on after I started going to church, Sam said something that wedged itself in my head good and hard. "Riddle me this, Abbie," he said. "If you're in so good with God now, why is it so fuckin' hard to make a baby?"

Don't get me wrong. I'm not trying to say Sam's an ogre. Don't think that. He's a good man, he really is. But whenever I would remember that for years after I would squeeze my fists until my nails drew blood.

I had to admit Sam had a point, though. We weren't doing a lot of begetting, no matter how often we had sex while I was ovulating or how many thousands we spent on treatments at the fertility clinic. All we wanted was a sweet little newborn and the only thing we had to show for our effort was a pile of medical bills.

When we first decided to go for it, it'd been so romantic. Sam would come to bed with a flower, or a little poem he'd written himself, that goofy grin on his face. And I'd wear my sexiest outfit, the lacy black camisole he'd had gotten me on our first anniversary, or sometimes I'd surprise him by wearing nothing at all under the cool sheets. It didn't take us long to get pregnant. Or so we thought.

When I missed my period we rushed to the drug store to buy

a home pregnancy test. Could hardly get home fast enough and pee on that little stick, and when it turned pink we were so happy. Went out to dinner at the steakhouse to celebrate. At the first doctor's visit that week they said everything was going well, and we started arguing over names. He wanted Andrew for a boy, I wanted Isabel for a girl.

We went back a month later for the ultrasound, wondering if we'd find out the sex that day. But in the examination room there was a problem. The technician had to go ask the doctor about something. She was gone a long time. When the doctor came in, she told us there was no embryo, just an empty sack. Anembryonic pregnancy, she called it. It couldn't have hurt worse if she'd plunged a knife right there into my jellied abdomen. I almost wished she had.

I didn't let Sam near me in bed for months after that. It just hurt too much.

I felt like such a piece of crap for so long. *Why can't I do this one thing any other woman can do?* I still felt like I had that knife in my abdomen. I could feel it twisting in my womb every day. And then I turned to God.

My friend Ellen invited me to the Assembly of God over on Pacific Street, and it all made sense right from the first visit. That day the preacher said we can't understand God's ways, but He has a reason for everything He does. And if there was a reason, it meant it wasn't my fault. As soon as I heard that my insides started to relax.

Not only that, but I realized God might only be testing me. If I just showed him how faithful I was maybe then he would finally let what I wished for come to pass.

I started praying all the time. I would just close my eyes and talk to God, didn't matter where. In the checkout line at the grocery store. Taking a shower. As soon as I woke up in the morning and before I went to bed. I tried so hard to be faithful, to be thankful, to be patient. I thought if only I accepted God's will, someday I would conceive. At night when everything was quiet and the only sound was Sam's even breathing, I would calm myself and listen, hoping maybe God would whisper back to me, telling me what to do.

I believed, I hoped, and I prayed, yet that one deepest desire I possessed did not come true. And all the while, Sam got more and more bitter. Mean even.

I shouldn't say that. It was as hard on him as it was on me. That was his way of dealing with it.

All his snide little comments sure didn't make things any easier for me, though. "Why don't you tell your Sky God to part these cars? You know, like the Red Sea," he said as we sat in his truck, simmering in a traffic jam on Dodge Street. Right, ha ha. And that night, like nothing had ever happened, he had the pure gall to kiss me on the cheek and say, "Maybe we should do it tonight, honey." Was I supposed to forget what he'd said earlier that day? But I did it anyway. I detested every second of it, but I let him roll on top of me and stick it in. I was his wife after all. Even with the comments and the hurtfulness, we were still trying to make it happen.

Anyway, I didn't let all that bother me too much. I was too involved at my new church. And I was so excited, so curious, learning new things every day about myself and my role in His plan. I read the Bible like it was a glass of water and I'd spent years in a desert. In a way, I had—an emotional desert. I didn't understand half of what I read, but that's not what mattered. The words just poured over me. Cooling, calming, soothing.

I wanted Sam to have the same peace I'd found. I asked him to come to church with me, but you can picture how that went over. "I would sooner pull my own fingernails out with pliers," he said. So I didn't ask again. Ever.

On my birthday, Sam took me to the Spaghetti Works in the Old Market, my favorite restaurant. He must have told the waiter about the occasion because at the end of the meal they brought a dish of hazelnut gelato and all the staff stood around the table clapping and singing "Happy Birthday." When they finished it was quiet for a second and I burst into tears. Somehow I'd gone all day without thinking about it, but it hit me right at that moment in the restaurant: I was forty-five. At that age you can pretty much write off ever getting pregnant. I knew right then I would really never have a baby of my own.

Everybody in the whole place turned around to see who was bawling on her birthday, probably expecting a five-year-old. I felt so bad, seeing the shocked look on Sam's face, but I couldn't help myself and cried and cried practically the whole way home in the truck.

He was so good about it. I apologized to him that night and he told me, "Hey, it's your party, you can cry if you want to." I laughed at that and he kissed me. I didn't turn away that time. I closed my eyes and let his lips press against mine, let his fingers run though my hair. Maybe that's why Sam didn't fly off the handle when I told him we had to move.

It came over me all of a sudden, a real conviction we were in the wrong place and had to go.

"But where we will we live? Where will we work?" Sam asked, sitting up in bed.

"The Lord will let us know when we get there," I said. The moving van was there that very weekend.

We got into town on Sunday and drove around, checking things out, with no real plan of where we would even spend the night. When we saw this place I knew instantly. The building was so tall and beautiful, and something about the gray stone and all the pinnacles and the pointed windows really struck me. It was like a cathedral, the kind of place where you could really get in contact with God. I said, "This is it," and Sam pulled the truck over. We went right in and signed a one-year lease for an apartment that was available immediately.

Our stuff arrived the next day. After hours of carrying boxes and furniture, sweaty and exhausted, I sat on a stool by the open window. The movers had left and all was peaceful outside in the courtyard, with hanging plants all around on people's balconies and the sky turning purplish with the coming night. I breathed in and the air smelled so fresh, filling my nostrils and lungs. And now I truly heard the Lord, and he was telling me it was time. I took off my clothes and went into the bedroom where Sam was unpacking a box of books and kissed him, fell right in his arms. We made love right there on the soft bare mattress, the first time in months. I knew right away a miracle had finally happened.

I was right, too. Nine months later I gave birth to Izzy, our gorgeous baby girl. She was born with a full head of curly brown hair and we brought her home to the nursery Sam and I had so carefully decorated with giraffes and lions and elephants.

She was so cute and precious, with her tiny fingers and the little pink booties we put on her feet. I never could understand why I was so sad all the time. More than that, I couldn't even muster the will to get out of bed. The feeling was so strong it was a physical weight holding me down. When I heard Izzy cry for me in the middle of the night, I groaned with all my soul. How could I be like this, when God had given me everything I had wanted? I would have been angry, except I couldn't even work up the emotion for that. Instead, I just hated myself. Hate was the only thing. The whole world seemed pointless and me most of all. I didn't deserve what I'd received.

Sam was so good during this time, feeding Izzy, playing with her, while her stupid Mommy just laid around all day. I thought it was a good sign when I became jealous of him, because she had become so attached to her Daddy. It meant I was starting to feel again. That encouraged me to pray, and with God's help, I became better gradually. I still had bad days, but they were fewer and farther between.

I insisted we raise her in the church, because God had done so much for us. That's when the second miracle occurred: Sam started coming with us. Probably he was humoring me, or maybe he'd had a genuine change of heart. I don't know. We went every week, and Sam and I listened to the sermon and held hands.

Now every morning I get up early for my own time with the Lord. I open the window and kneel with my arms on the sill, breathing in His good air and thanking Him for all He has provided for my family. The two miracles that have changed my life. The Lord talks back too. Not in words, but in the way I feel in my soul. So close to Him, in touch with his loving nature. I could not imagine a happier, more fulfilled life.

Izzy had her third birthday two weeks ago exactly. She's at the age now where she has a mind of her own. She insisted she wanted a birthday cake with princesses, so I bought one at the grocery store and invited a few of her friends from daycare over. We held the party in the courtyard, put the cake on the picnic table made of white stone.

After Izzy blew out the candles, Sam picked up the stainless steel knife to cut the cake. His hand brushed the hand of one of the mothers. He smiled at her and she smiled back, her brown eyes flickering as if it wasn't their first touch. I nearly fell to the ground in shock, a rush of blood to my head reminding me of the bad. All those years we couldn't conceive. Sam's hateful remarks. The way I'd felt it was my fault all that time for not getting pregnant. My tears that night at the restaurant. Even those dark days after Izzy was born when I acted so ungrateful.

I was nearly overtaken by panic right there in the courtyard. Were things really different now, between us? How well did he know this other woman? How many times had they met? Maybe I didn't even truly deserve his love, or a beautiful child, or a happy life. At that moment in my mind, it was as if the last several years hadn't taken place at all.

"Honey, are you all right?" Sam asked.

I took a deep breath, got ahold of myself. "I'm fine," I said. "I was just a little dizzy for a second." I picked up the matchbook and saw that my palms were bloody.

The next morning I opened my eyes and the crushing feeling hit me. It was another of those days like after Izzy was born. I forced myself to get out of bed and open the window. I kneeled down and breathed in the air. It wasn't fresh anymore, or warm or sweet. It was cold and sharp as needles in my lungs, my gut, down to my womb. And I knew right away it meant the Lord was asking me to do something. Something I didn't want to do.

I had to kill Izzy.

I closed the window and went back to bed. Tears ran down my face as I laid there. When Sam woke up he asked me if something was wrong. I told him I didn't feel well, that was all.

I went over it in my mind, considered it from every angle. Why would God do this? Maybe it was mercy. Maybe something was wrong with Izzy, and killing her now would save her from suffering later. I watched her all day for signs of illness, but she seemed so healthy and happy, running to the swings at the playground and shouting in her little voice, "Mommy! Mommy! Push me!"

Three days I opened that window in the mornings, and three days that cold air entered me. I prayed to Him, I pleaded with Him. I prostrated myself on the floor and opened myself to Him, hoping that if He could only see how faithful I was He wouldn't lay that terrible command on my heart. But in the end, I knew God wasn't changing his mind.

On the fourth day I waited until Sam went to work. I picked out the stainless steel carving knife from our wooden knife block, the same one he had used on the cake, and placed it in a tote bag. I called Izzy to me and kissed her on the cheek and told her we were going down to the courtyard. She took my hand and we went out the door.

I hoped the elevator would stop on the way down, that somebody would get in and grab me and put a stop to it, maybe that old janitor who was always hanging around. No one did. The door opened and I led Izzy down the corridor.

"Where are we going, Mommy?" she asked.

"To the courtyard."

"Are we going to play there?"

"Mommy has something she has to do there."

"Did you bring a snack, Mommy?"

I squeezed her hand harder and pushed through the double glass doors into the courtyard. There in the center stood the stone table. I picked Izzy up and sat her on top.

"Lie down and close your eyes, Izzy."

"It's not my naptime, Mommy!"

"Let's pretend it is."

She laid down and closed her eyes, smiling in anticipation of the fun game we were about to play. I took out the knife from the bag and gripped it in my right hand, covering her eyes with my other. I raised the knife and did not hesitate, because I had prepared myself in my mind for this moment. I put my faith in the Lord and trusted in His will. I brought the blade down in a smooth, clean motion, and as it was about to pierce her ribcage a voice shouted, "Stop!"

I jerked my hand back and looked around. Nobody was there.

"What are you doing, Mommy?" Izzy asked, her eyes open now.

"Nothing, baby," I said, checking the windows on the upper floors. Where had the voice come from? "Let's go back inside."

I replaced the knife in the bag and brought Izzy back upstairs. Inside the apartment the window was open. Odd, I was positive I had shut it earlier, because the air was so cold. Now though, the sun was out and I started to sweat, big oily drops oozing down my face. The sweat ran off me onto the floor. It was as if somebody had pulled a plug, and all the anger and pain I'd built up for years drained out of me, right out in a black puddle by the coffee table.

Izzy laughed. "You're all wet, Mommy!" I stumbled to a chair and sat and held her in my lap. I felt relief, as if I had passed a test I hadn't even known I was taking. And although I still pray every morning, it's been two weeks now and God hasn't spoken to me since.

THE INN OF ROUGH TIMBERS

The most recently written of the stories in this volume, The Inn of Rough Timbers *will appear in the forthcoming 2023 Writers of Chantilly anthology,* Did I Ever Tell You About the Time…? *This one was inspired by the anthology's theme, of course, but also (rather like* La Jolla Ballroom*) by a list of 18th century British criminal slang I found online.*

It was some years ago when the events I'm about to relate took place, when I was a much younger and bolder man than I am now. Indeed, I should not now venture into a region with such a reputation for lawlessness, but at the time I had that sense common to all young men of being immune somehow to the possibility of misfortune or even death. And in my line of work, I had reason to believe that there was some wealth to be won in commercial dealings with certain traders known to me in the main town of that far-flung district, a place I had not been for many years and have not returned to since.

I left the town in haste, and the landscape soon changed from rolling grassy hills to a more rugged, nearly mountainous woods of steep inclines and rocky outcroppings. It was one of those years when the cold comes early to those northern parts, the frost-touched winds whipping through my clothes as if the sky itself conspired to keep me off the path, the rain cutting across my face as bitter and burning to my flesh as any bellows-blown flame. My horse had the worst of it, of course, contending not only with the elements but with my own urging him on at speed along the dim wooded paths. But he bore it without complaint, hoping as I did, I suppose, to reach quickly some place of comfort and warmth. The evening approached and our light faded rapidly, and I dreaded to think of having to spend the night in the open in those unwelcoming, and according to rumor, ruffian-infested woods.

Never mind my business being in those parts so late in the year, and at such an unpropitious time of day. Suffice it to say, my dealings in town had gone badly, and I was in a foul mood and with no desire to stay another moment in that ugly, cursed little burg where so much had befallen me. So heedless of the warnings of my business associates both as to the weather and the dangers of the road, I had set out as soon as it became apparent we would not reach terms on the proposition at hand, though at their insistence, I did consent to carry a pistol in a pocket inside my cloak. I had thought to attain some village or house of hospitality by nightfall, but I was not familiar with that country and had badly misjudged its wildness and the scantiness of its conveniences.

Indeed, I had suspected for some time I had lost the path itself, and was contemplating the disagreeable prospect of turning back and trying to reestablish our way. Thus, it was with no small relief that just as the light was about to dwindle to nothing, my horse and I came of a sudden over a ridge and out of the trees, arriving in a little clearing with a rude wooden house and several outbuildings. The house was of rough-hewn timbers, grayed with age and bereft of paint or ornament, but it seemed built tight enough to keep out the elements, at least. Perhaps under different circumstances I would have hesitated to enter such an establishment. But I could hardly care about the roughness of the construction on that night; I was grateful just to see smoke rising from the chimneys, and a groom waiting on a chair under an overhang on the front of the main building, safely out of the rain.

I wasted no time in giving the lad a whistle, slipping him a coin, with a promise of more if he took particular care with my mount. As the boy led him off, I could sense my horse was as grateful as I for the prospect of a dry night with a bit of food to fill an empty stomach. I pushed through the door with the pleasant expectation of the cheer and good company usual to such country inns. I received then my first inkling of what I had gotten myself into.

As soon as I entered, all conversation ceased. The place, though small, was packed full enough. Half a dozen large tables and numerous small ones jammed the dining room, each occupied by patrons crowded shoulder to shoulder, shoveling their suppers from trenchers and slurping from tankards, their knives and cups froze to observe me as I stood by the door, stamping the wet off my boots. Bewhiskered, hard-eyed men with dark faces as weathered as the building's timbers stared me down, matched by sullen women with faces hardly less furrowed than their menfolk.

A stooped woman of advanced age squeezed her way among the chairs and tables from the open entryway to the kitchen. The crackle of a flame in the stone fireplace, her shuffling steps across the floor, and the scrape of chair legs across the floorboards were the only sounds. *Ah, here then's the proprietress,* I thought, removing my cloak and holding it out.

"A seat, if you please," I said. "And a supper as well."

She did not take my proffered offering, but let it drip, keeping a pace away as her rheumy eyes scrutinized me up and down. When she responded, her voice squawked as if she was not used to speaking out. "How found ye this place?"

I laughed uneasily. "Why, do travelers along the path not stop here when they pass by? Although I must own, between the clouds and the season's early sunset, I scarcely had faith I had kept to the path a'tall."

"So ye come here alone?" she asked.

"Indeed," I replied. On an attempted jovial note, I added, "Except for my loyal steed."

"Hnn." The woman's non-committal, almost grunting response seemed the signal for the company to fall back to their suspended conversations and meals. The tense moment passed and she consented then to take my cloak and hung it on a hook near the door, the only one not occupied already by the outerwear of the other guests. She pinched the fabric of my sleeve and led me to a single small table I had not previously noticed in a back corner.

"A penny for supper and ale," she squawked at me. "Or two pence for strong ale."

I was taken aback to be asked for payment in advance, but reasoned that travelers obviously being so rare in those parts, strangers must be little trusted. In any case, I indulged the queer, suspicious custom, and took two pennies from my coinpurse to place in her swollen-knuckled hand. She clutched the coins and retreated into the kitchen.

I pulled out my pipe and tobacco, tamping it into the pipe bowl. As I did, I took the opportunity to survey the room, though a closer inspection hardly changed the opinion I had formed at my first impression. The crowd was rough and mean, the conversations low-toned and edgy, and I noticed many a hand hidden in a sleeve or under a fold of clothing, as if poised to grasp a concealed dagger or other weapon. The commerce between the men and women had none of that affection or good-natured teasing usual in such places, and the clear deference of the women to their husbands or paramours had not an air of modest obedience, but rather of tired acquiescence or meek submission, as a dog will display before an unkind master. At one table, a dour party played a game of cards with little apparent amusement, but with wary eyes and growled admonitions to "play your turn already, Bill," or "watch I don't catch you slipping that hidden jack in the deck."

But soon it was the occupants of the very table closest to me that attracted my attention. There were three gentlemen, if I may use the term loosely, seated there, and apparently well into their cups. What drew my notice was their boisterous conversation. Indeed, they seemed the only spirited fellows in the place. For though the noise of the crowd was considerable, it was due more to the sheer number of its members and the closeness of the seating, than any liveliness on the part of the speakers.

These men, however, engaged in animated talk such that I was able to hear their intercourse quite clearly.

"I tells you, lads," one of them was saying, a small, wiry man with the most notable feature of a line of raised, pink scars around his neck, as from a rope. His voice rasped like paper on paper. "'Twas the richest trio of riders one like to come across. Breeches with silver buckles and ruffled lace and finery. Splendid, they was, and loaded too. My greatest capture, if I do say so meself."

"Eh?" one of his companions said, leaning in for the story. "Do tell, then, Davy. Let's hear of it."

"Why, it happened so," said Davy, rubbing his hands with anticipatory relish at the story he was about to relate. "I was hiding at the curve in the highway near Johnson's gulch. I believe you know the spot."

"Indeed so, go on," his companions urged.

"When I heard the horses' hooves, I figured on the mail, and you know how long it's been since the mail passed by without an escort. But then I spotted these three coming a-riding, an older and two younger fellows, and the younger ones all macaroni with wig and short coat, and I says to myself, 'Davy, this is a chance that come along only rarely, and not to be passed up.' So I pulled out my coat pistol and dropped into the road."

"And they didn't rush by on their horses?" one of the others asked. "If, as you say, it was only you."

"Aye, but how was they to know that?" Davy said. "So I drops in front of them and I cries, "halt!" and I waves the popper and acts for all the world like I've got a whole gang in the trees just waiting. And they comes to a stop and I gives 'em a show. 'I got me lads in the woods,' I says, 'and a more blood-thirsty bunch you never seen. But it don't have to come to all that. Just hand over your valuables and we can all get on.'

"Well, the older fellow and one of the younger ones, they're pale and shaking and already has their hands in their coats to pull out their purses. But the one younger one, the old man's son, as I suppose it—" Davy shook his head here in admiration—"he's got a pair of gingamobs the size of apples on him, he does. For he reaches in his coat as well, but withdraws not a purse but a pistol as he cries, 'I don't believe you,' and afore I knows it, I'm staring down the barrel of his firearm. 'Put your purse away, Father,' he says. 'This brigand will be taking nothing from us today.'"

"Ha!" one of the companions said. "No hen-hearted traveler, he!"

"Indeed not," Davy said drily. "So there we were, both of us with our poppers pointed one at the other, he on the horse and I on the ground, and no more than five paces from the other. It was then I had my piece of luck."

He paused here to let his companions urge him on, which they did, to his evident gratification. "Yes, what was it, Davy? Tell, tell!"

"Why, at that moment, at that exact moment, a branch fell from a tree in the woods. Created an awful cracking, it did. Couldn't have timed it better if I'd wanted to. And that was all the evidence the son needed, for he took it to be one of my gang. Turned white as shirt, the young fellow did. And I didn't let the opportunity go a-wasting, let me tell you."

By now, Davy's fellows were turning red with laughter as they envisioned the scene. "And, what happened then?" they said.

"Well, the other young one, the brother, as I take it, he cries out, 'Mortimer, give the man the money. It be not worth our lives!'

"And I adds on, 'You should listen to your brother, Mortimer. I'm an impatient man, and though I don't want no bloodshed on this road, you best not try my patience.' And young Mortimer, I could tell how it galled him to do it, but he puts the popper back in his coat, and pulls out his purse. And they all three toss their purses to my feet.

"I bend over, pick up one of the purses, and open one up. I knows the pay-off was rich, for the purse was full to the top with crowns and guineas. And just to keep the show going, I walk over, real slow-like, and I waggles my finger—" here he waggled his finger, as if biding someone to come closer—"and I says in a low voice, 'Listen to this.' So Mortimer leans over off his nag, and…." He tailed off and grinned wolfishly.

"Well, well?" came the pleadings of his companions.

"And I smacks Mortimer hard on his face, open hand, like you might with one of these wenches in here." He nodded generally in the direction of the rest of the crowd. His interlocutors howled with mirth.

"Oh, I could tell Mortimer burned," he continued when the laughter died down, "and the outline of my fingers glowed red on his cheek. How he stared me down! But he daren't do a goddamn thing about it, with my gang in the woods and all. So then I call into the woods, 'Alright lads, let 'em pass.' And I wave the riders on. And that, my friends, is how I robbed three mounted, armed travelers all alone, and with nary a drop of blood spilt, by the by."

At this conclusion, the three all fairly collapsed in merriment and laughter, and there was a good deal of back-slapping as well, and they called out "Betty, another round of strong ale." I couldn't help but notice the proprietress attended to them far faster than she had to me. As she brought their tankards, another of the fellows clapped the table, this one a well-tricked gent overtopped with curly, dark hair, a huge veiny nose, a swarthy complexion, and most notably, a fine black mustache curved and pointed as the Ottomans wear it.

"Davy, that was quite a tale," the swarthy fellow said. "Aye, that be a tale to remember indeed. And I daresay Mortimer 'taint forgotten it! But I do admit, I think I can top ye."

Davy raised his eyebrows and ran his fingers along those raw pink scars along his neck. "Why, George, don't be modest. If you have a story that can best mine, let's hear it."

So George took a long pull from his tankard and wiped his mouth with his sleeve. And the other two leaned in the better to hear him, and I did as well, though doing my best to appear I wasn't listening a'tall.

"Now the way this story starts, is that I was at Missus Pennypacker's public stew over in P____," he said, mentioning the very town I had left that day.

"Aye, exactly how every story should start!" interjected his companions.

"Just so, just so," George said. "But not the way you think. For 'twas winter, and the fireplaces was roaring, and all the men and the ladies of the house were huddled around it for warmth, and so cold nobody getting up except to go warm themselves another way, if you know what I mean. But that was how I heard about the score.

"For it happened there was one of those times that you sometimes reach in a group where all are talking at once, a point where the talk ceases and all is quiet, except for one remaining conversation, which becomes revealed and naked, as it were, without the clothing of the other talk to cover it. And we were all so a-pressed together that you could hear even the whispers between two lovers. And that's when I heard a gloak discoursing with his paramour, and he said the words, '...tomorrow on the noon at Drowned Child's Pond. Just don't say me name aloud when you get there.'

"Now I heard these words most distinct, and anybody else there that night must have assumed the two made some arrangements for a tryst, insofar as they paid any attention to the words a'tall. But to you and you and me—" he pointed here to the other two— "we know that the Royal Post passes over the footbridge at Drowned Child's Pond twice a week at just that time. So I reckoned on a robbery.

"And the more I considered it, the more sense it made, for indeed the next day was Tuesday, a post day. And with the weather being cold as it was, who would meet at the footbridge, outdoors and miles from the city, to meet a lover? No, a robbery it had to be, and the two of them must've somehow come into some information that there would be something rich in the next day's mail. And so a plan began to hatch in me mind."

George paused for a long draft of his ale, wiping the suds from his mustache when he was done. The other two urged him on.

"Aye, aye, and a brilliant plan it was, too. For I knew it would not just be the two of them to conduct a robbery, not of the Royal Post, and one of them a woman. No, it had to be a whole pack of which they was just two. Now I wanted that prize they must be after, but how to get it? I could intercept the mail a-fore it reached the footbridge of course, but how could one man carry off a robbery like that? Of course, I hadn't heard Davy's tale yet at that time." The companions broke out into general laughter at that.

"But then I conceived of another way. For, you see, I realized the key was the second thing the lover had said: 'Don't say me name aloud.' For that meant the robbers *weren't known to one another.* Do y'see? We've all participated in such a no-name job, so if one is caught he mightn't rat out the others and lead the whole lot to the sheriff's picture frame. What's more, considering the situation and the temperature, it was a fair bet all were going to be masked.

"And then I became really excited, for to go to the trouble of a no-name job meant the prize must be rich, indeed. And that's when the idea struck me like a hammer on a bell."

He paused to stroke the pointy tips of his mustache and grinned. "Well, well?" the other two urged.

"I would show up and take over the job. You see? I would present myself as the boss. For with each unknown to the others, who could say for sure?"

The other two exhaled in unison. But then Davy interjected, "And what happens when the real boss shows up? He weren't like to share his position."

"Why then," George replied with a sly look. "I shoot him down. And all the better, for who then would among the others would contradict me?"

"But George," the third man said. "You claim that the whore was to show up as well. Now, how could it be a robbery if the man were to take his betsy along to it?"

"Why, she was to be the maid in distress, of course." George lifted an eyebrow. "To distract the post riders. How else would they stop riders on the footbridge? I reckoned whoever was in charge had it all planned it out, and real clever-like, too. And all I needs do was ease myself in, and ease the other fellow out.

"So I set out early the next day with me own mask and a brace of poppers in me belt, headed for Drowned Child's Pond so as to arrive afore the others. The sun was out but the day was as cracking cold as any I can remember. The ice on the pond must have been so thick the fish was standing still in the water, if you see what I mean.

"I stood shivering off in a stand of trees a-waiting. Just as I suspected, it weren't long 'til they start showing up, hiding themselves all around the pond in the bushes and whatnot. You might never have seen 'em if you didn't know they were there, but once you knew to look, you could spot each man in his mask, and all stamping and blowing on their hands to keep warm. Not long before noon, the harlot herself shows up, and she's done up as innocent a virgin as you please. Why, with the modesty of her clothes, and her hair tied back with a simple ribbon, and only the cold of the air to redden her cheeks instead of rouge, anyone who didn't know better might have taken her for a maiden of the right stamp.

"She takes her place on the footbridge, and when the sound of horses' hooves come in the distance, she starts rubbing her eyes so's to make it look as though she's been weeping. Now here comes the mail coach, pulled by two horses and with a driver and a guard in the king's uniform, and you can wager another guard in the coach. The slattern sets her elbows on the railing and puts her head in her hands, as though in distress. Of course, the driver calls the horses to a stop as they're crossing. The guard stands in the box and puts his hand to his pistol, sensing it might be a ruse.

"'Good morning, Miss,' the driver calls. 'Is there some trouble?"

"'It's my fiancé," the girl cried, and the quaver she put in her voice made even my heart tremble for her. 'I was to meet him here at eleven o'clock, but I fear he's been waylaid.'

"'Aye,' the driver says. 'It be likely in these parts. But how come you to be a-waiting on him here at this spot? This 'taint no place for a young miss.'

"'Because of my father,' she says, dramatic as could be. 'He doesn't approve of my fiancé. So we were to meet here and *run away together*,' and her voice cracked and she started in with the tears. Now it was those words that must have been the signal, for I observed that the men in hiding came out and approached either end of the bridge, but all quiet-like. And the harlot is weeping and sniffling and carrying-on as a distraction, so that the driver and guard never saw the approaching danger. I figured it was time for me to make my entrance.

"So I rise and push past the men at the closest end of the bridge and march right up the planks with a bulldog in each hand and two more loaded in me belt. The harlot sees me and her eyes widen and she turns pale, for this warn't the way the plan was supposed to go, but I got me own plans. And of course I spoiled their element of surprise, for the guard has his popper out now and trained on me, and as I thought he lets out a whistle and another guard opens the coach door and steps down with his popper, too. But I laugh at them and say, 'Put away your firearms, lads, for you're outnumbered five to one.'

"I indicated the men on either side of the bridge, and all around the pond as well, pointing each one out in his hiding place and bidding them rise, that the king's men might get a look at them. They were hesitant, for this sure warn't what they'd rehearsed, but they did as I said.

"'You see?' I says to the driver and guards. 'There's no way out for you. But if you surrender, we'll let you live. All we want is what you have in the coach.'

"I could tell the guard on the front of the coach warn't going to have it, for his lip curled and he readied to speak. But that warn't even my main concern just then, for from behind me I hear footsteps a-stomping up the planks, no doubt the old Robin what's in charge of this whole business, and without turning I knowed he was looking like God's revenge against murther.

"Well, lads, if I warn't to be shot in the front then I was to be shot in the back, and I didn't have a second spare." Here George took a pause for a long drink from his tankard, and he set it down and leaned back in his seat so the front two legs of the chair rose off the floor, as if he was considering whether to go on.

The other two leaned forward. "Well, well, don't leave us in suspense," they cried as one. "Tell what happened next?"

George smiled and slowly rocked forward again. He put his elbows on the table and inhaled deeply. "What happened next? Why, I snabbed 'em."

"Who, who?"

"The whole lot!"

"The whole lot?" asked the companions.

"The whole lot," George roared with a slap on the table. "I sent 'em all straight to the eternity box. Here's how it happened, lads: shot one, I fired my popper at the guard on the front of the coach and caught him right in his puddings. Shot two, I ducked and whirled and hit the old Robin. I tossed those two poppers away and pulled the two out me belt, whirling again. All this in under a second, mind. I hit the guard on the side of the coach and he dropped. When she saw the old Robin fall, the harlot started in to screaming, so the final shot was for her."

"You shot the whore?" Davy said, his jaw dropping.

"That's what I said, ain't it?" George replied, as cool as you like. "The whole bridge was folks a'falling kickerapoo. And at the end it was just the driver and me. 'I think it's best if you let loose those reins and come down off the box,' I says to him, and he does just what I tells him. At that point, the whole band of robbers has no idea what just happened, but they don't dare contradict me. For all they knows, I'm the real boss of the thing anyhow. We tie up the driver, unload the coach, and divide it up amongst us, and let me tell you, it was no fiddler's money. 'Twas crowns, shiny and new, and all the gold and silver coins you like, and banknotes too, enough to warm the heart of any topping man."

"But what did you do with the bodies?" the third man asked.

"Why, we threw 'em on the ice!" George said. "I suppose they stayed there until spring when it warmed up enough for 'em to sink and feed the fishes!"

At that, all three of the companions laughed heartily, and now the third fellow leaned forward, for it was his turn. He was a lean, angular man with a protruding Adam's apple and a calculating eye, and given to strange, jerky gesticulations with one hand while he spoke, as if to fend off flying pests only he could see.

"Davy, George." He nodded at the other two in turn. "Ye've both said enough to make a dog laugh. But now I'll tell ye a real tale."

"If you can top George's story, there's a guinea in it, Rees," Davy said.

When I heard that curious name "Rees," my gut turned as chill as the greasy, uneaten mutton stew the proprietress had placed before me. Finally I apprehended who it was I was listening in on. Davy, with the raised scars around his neck? Why, 'twas none other than Twice-Hanged Davy, wanted from Worcester to Norwich and many places in between. George? This must be the notorious Turkish George, known almost as much for his swarthy complexion and fine mustache as his violent disposition and escapes from gaol in multiple shires. And finally, Rees. Surely this could be none other than Rees the Snook: wanted by no fewer than a dozen sheriffs for highway robbery, murther, and a raft of other offenses against the King's law, as well. The three most notorious highwaymen in the land, at the next table over from me, no less.

What's more, as I glanced again around the establishment, I saw those hard, merciless faces with newly understanding eyes. The way I'd lost the trail, only to have apparently regained it and come across an inn? Why, I'd never regained the trail at all. Only by sheerest misfortune had I come across this place, this inn of rough timbers, intentionally located where no one would find it who didn't already know its location. For these men drinking and eating around me so sullenly were the highwaymen and footpads, cutthroats and counterfeiters, lackeys, abetters, and general rogues of that whole disreputable district. How malevolent every stray laugh, every whisper, every murmur suddenly seemed to me!

As I considered all this, my heart quailing with the new knowledge, Rees proceeded with his tale. "Lads, I've no need to tell ye the richest folks in P____ are all Tremblers. They've got some queer habits to be sure, but I reckon the Lord must smile on them for it, as all the money flows to them. Well, let me tell you of a time that the Devil smiled on me, for I came across the information that a certain Trembler merchant was to make a purchase of his materials for a whole year, and was to pay for 'tall in gold."

"Now Rees," Turkish George said, steepling his fingers on the table. "How'd you find this out? Every mother's son knows if there's one thing a Trembler likes less than spending chink, it's opening their mouths to jaw. And they hardly do business, except with each other."

"Never you mind where I found it out," Rees replied. "And if you try any more such impertinence you'll get a knife through your palm for your trouble." Here Rees made a sudden diving wave with his right hand, which was in the air already to illustrate the story with his wild motions. Turkish George jumped back in his seat, withdrawing his hands from the tabletop as if Rees really held a knife.

"As I was saying," Rees continued, "this particular Trembler lived in a fine house in the center of town, and I won't say his name but if I did ye'd both know him, and the house as well, for its fineness is a-famed, or was anyways, before the big fire in twenty-six. When I heard the information about the gold, I racked me brains for how to get ahold of it. Like ye two, I mulled over all sorts of schemes for robbing the horses on the way. But as I thought and thought, finally I settled on a plan of true daring. Y'see, I realized the real money was not merely what might be on the road for an hour or a day, but what was in the man's house. Imagine the wealth he must have stored away in that place! But 'twas the payment for the materials that would give me access."

"Ah, clever, clever," Twice-Hanged Davy said. "Why pluck the tail-feather when you can grab the whole goose?"

"Indeed," Rees said. "So on the appointed day, I knocked upon his door in the late morning, knowing the delivery was to take place that afternoon. I had dressed meself in the Trembler fashion, all brown and gray, and with the wrap to cover my head, as they believe shows them humble under the eye of God. When he opened the door—which he did himself, as hiring manservants and butlers and such is forbidden them—I says to him, in the Trembler way, 'Good day, Brother, and greetings to you from Samuel and Josiah,' for such were the names of the men who were to make the delivery.

"And to me, he says, 'Good day to you, Brother, but pray tell me where my cousins be and how you came to be here at my door?' And I gives him my whole story, which I'd rehearsed ahead of time, making sure to use the proper Trembler words, explaining about his cousins being detained by the bishop in S____bury, but sending me on, a friend in the underground church in that town, to make the delivery in their stead. And this was the stroke of genius, you see, for the bishop of S___bury be known for his hatred of the Tremblers, and not suffering a Trembler to appear in his town, on pain of a week in the blockhouse and a visit to the flogging stake. So now the owner of the house was worked up with worry for his cousins and how he might aid them, and he hardly gave a thought to me a'tall.

"Now courtesy required him to introduce me to his wife and children, and I greeted them the expected way, as 'Goodwife So-and-So,' and the children, seven of them, with all the little girls named 'Purity' and 'Chastity' and other such nonsense, and a couple older boys called 'Hezekiah' and 'Bezaleel' and I don't know what. After that came the part I'd been waiting for, when he took me to his closet within his private chamber, where he kept his desk and his iron-bound chests, unlocking it with a key from his vest. I presented to him a sample of the supply he was to buy, which of course I'd bought earlier from a merchant in town. But he barely checked it, his thoughts with his cousins and how he could aid them in their troubles, asking me constantly if I thought he should ride to S___bury, or what he might do.

"So I simply slip into the conversation that of course I must check that he's good for the payment, which as I understood, was to be paid in gold. He nodded and opened one of the chests, and I could hardly keep me eyes in me head, for 'twas filled to the brim with five-guineas and silver crowns. And I tell ye, lads, that was just one chest of five." Rees paused in his tale and his eyes shone with the memory.

"So what'd you do then?" Turkish George prompted.

"Why, I drubbed him with an oaken towel on the spot," Rees said. "For I'd made sure me walking stick was good and stout, and I waited until he bent over, and struck him on the mazzard. He tried to rise to his feet, all shaky and buffle-headed, but I gave him another crack and he dropped to the floor.

"'Twas a job well-done, but now I had to spirit away the body somehow, not to mention explain what had happened to Goodwife So-and-So. And indeed, already she was calling back, 'John, John, is all well?' And before I could think how to warn her off somehow, she poked her head in the closet and sees her husband laid out on the floor with the blood running out from his nob and started in with the blubbering."

"Ha!" cried Twice-Hanged Davy. "A spot we all well know. How'd you shut her bone box?"

"Nothing for it but to give her a knock as well," Rees said. "So now, *two* bodies, a passel of kids who all knows my face, and Samuel and Josiah on the way, perhaps within the hour. How was I to remove the chests and dispose of the bodies before they arrived?

"I racked my brains, I tell ye, with how to dispose of those bodies and the evidence to boot. But then a notion took me. Why get rid of the bodies a'tall? Perhaps I could play this to my advantage. So I fish around in John's vest until I finds the key, and I shuts the closet up. And I go off to explain to the older boys that their father and mother had to go out on an errand, but would be back in good time."

Turkish George raised an eyebrow. "And the squeakers believed your story? Even after the sounds of the scuffle?"

"Why, George, I don't think you understand the attitude of a Trembler," Rees said. "They're trained up from childhood to trust one another. That's why they can do business together so easy. And why not, for they're all square fellows, t'ain't they? Now mind, I wore the clothes of a Trembler. And I had taken on the speech of a Trembler, as well, filling me talk with 'Should God will its' and 'May the Lord bless its' and suchlike. It never even came into their nobs not to trust me. Not the squeakers, and not the grown-folk neither.

"So as I said, I told the older boys their parents had gone out and they was to make me comfortable with a bit of refreshment from the kitchen while I waited. When they was out back in the kitchen, I dragged the iron-bound chests from the closet to the private chamber. When they came with my repast I ate in a hurry and after—on their father's order, I said to the boys—we carried those chests out to the front court. Nor was they light to hold, but the boys proved hardy and diligent as you expect from Trembler youths, and having not a clue that what they held was the very wealth of their household.

"Then I went back to their father's chamber, and said, if Samuel and Josiah was to come while I waited, they should bring them in to see me, for their father wished me to conduct his business while he was absent.

"So of course, Samuel and Josiah comes a-knocking at the door to the very minute of when they was expected, and the two older boys sees them in just as I asked 'em to. And at first I exchanges the Trembler greetings with the two, wishing them blessings and inquire after their families and so forth, and I explain I'm acting as an agent for the owner of the house, who's away for the day. But when the talk turns to business, soon I contrive to stir up a point of contention, a difference on the price of the supplies they have waiting outside, accusing them of changing the terms. It all becomes heated, and our voices rise and Josiah and Samuel gets all red in the face, and I make sure we're loud enough for the children to hear. Then, I opens up the closet and shows them in, but without lighting the candle first, and as soon as they're in I slip out quick-like and lock the door.

"Well, then it's a matter of simplicity." Rees's gesticulations grew excited as he explained his cleverness. "For I first goes and send the boys off on some small errand so they're out of the house, but to return in a few minutes. When they get back, I tell the boys something terrible has happened, there's been a row, of which they are in no doubt, having earlier heard the voices. I explain that their parents came home while they were gone and went in to work out the business deal with Josiah and Samuel, who were in a state of vexation, and the row continued, and even came to fisticuffs. And then I takes them back and lights a candle and opens the closet, and Samuel and Josiah come stumbling out, angered at how I mistreated them, and blustering and flustering, and when all see the dead bodies laid out on the floor, there comes a proper deep hush.

"Samuel and Josiah could deny all they like, but by now I have the boys on my side, and I bade them fetch the watch. Now when the watchmen come, of course the story's all muddled, but it's me and the boys on the one side, and two strangers from another city on the other, so the watch quods Samuel and Josiah in the block-house, figuring to let the judge work out the particulars."

"But Rees," Davy said. "What good does all that do you? For the true story must come out before the judge and then you're hanged."

"Aye," Rees replied. "But unlike you, Davy, I prefer to make my escapes *before* the noose is around my neck. Ye see, I'm free and the Tremblers is not. So I have those iron-bound chests on the very wagon Josiah and Samuel brought with them, loaded with the help of the boys. I'm out of the city gates before any are the wiser to how it really happened. The chests are hid good and safe and the wagon run deep in the river, and me knee deep in Eve's customhouse at a stew miles away. That's how 'tis done proper, lads!"

Rees's grin at the conclusion of his story brought gales of laughter from the three comrades, but it set my heart to cold fury. I put away my pipe, and as I'd paid for my supper at the beginning, there was nothing holding me there except the cold and wind I knew awaited me outside. But I was determined not to spend another moment in such company. I pushed my chair back and inconspicuously made my way to the front door, taking up my cloak over my arm in preparation to put it on.

But as I was about to don the cloak before exiting, I heard a voice rasp behind me. "And where is it you're off to at this late hour?"

I whirled and there was Twice-Hanged Davy, with George and Rees behind him, George's mustache all a-quiver and Rees gesticulating like he was conducting a brass band. The inn was silent as a tomb, and my guts froze to ice. But I kept myself outwardly calm. "I've eaten my supper," I said. "And now I intend to be on my way."

"Not after what you've heard." Rees's voice was low and dangerous, and his hand strayed inside his pocket. "You think we weren't flash to you sitting there, listening in on our private discourse?"

"I hardly heard a word," I said. "Sounded like a lot of tittle-tattle to me."

"Did it now?" George said. "But we sure would hate for you to repeat our tittle-tattle to the law."

"I know how to keep mum," I replied. But I saw that my reassurances had little effect, for the three highwaymen advanced slowly upon me, and there was murther in their faces. In that tight little house, there was no way for me to reach the door before they set upon me.

Now, as I said, my cloak was over my arm, and it so happened that my hand was practically at the opening of that inner pocket where my business associates earlier that day had insisted I stow a pistol for the road. Making as if to spread my cloak over my shoulders, and simultaneously wave away the concerns of the three men as insignificant, I thrust my hand entirely inside the pocket and grabbed the gun's handle, swinging the cloak around to disguise my movements.

For a moment the cloak spread in the air, blocking the view between them and me, and as I spun toward the door I fired at where Rees stood, but when the cloak settled around my shoulders and I glanced back, it was Turkish George who staggered, blood spreading across his fine lace shirt.

Davy turned to his companion, but Rees leapt at me, one hand glinting in the lamplight with a wicked little blade. Now in my line of work, this was not my first time to encounter ruffians such as these, and indeed, I had a bit of training in the art of pugilism. So rather than step back, as most men would instinctually, and as he expected, I stepped forward to meet his body, and at the same time thrust away his stabbing hand with my left forearm, and striking his puddings with my right fist. His mouth parted in surprise at the blow, and the knife clattered to the floor.

I had some thought to stay and finish the job I'd started with Rees, but now motion rippled through the crowd, and as the sound of chairs scraping against floorboards reached my ears, it seemed to me wisest to use the few seconds I had bought for myself to be on my way. I opened the latch and stepped out in the night, giving a whistle for the lad.

And now I had some luck, for the door opened outward, and the boards of the porch were so rough-hewn that when the boy hopped up from his chair, I realized I could take it and jam its legs in a crack in the boards, and wedge its back under the door latch, and thus bottle up the tumult inside the house, so to speak. It would hold at least until the chair splintered, for already the denizens pounded the door against the obstruction.

"My horse, boy! Do you remember which one it was?"

The coin I'd tossed him earlier had its effect, for he cried, "Aye, sir," took up the lantern, and set himself to run off.

But on a sudden notion that arose in my head, I cried, "Wait!" He stopped on the threshold of the stair and glanced back at me with a curious look. He could hear the rising clamor as well as I and knew that something was afoot.

"Have you any relations in the house?" I asked.

"Relations, sir?"

"Relations…a mother, a father?"

"Why, yes, sir," he said. "My uncle is in the house."

"Ah, I see," I replied, dismissing my idea.

"But I hates him," the lad added hastily. "He drubs me with his belt if I forget to sweep the kitchen, and sometimes if I don't. He makes me wait out here in the cold while he's in the warm, and if I dast complain, he bastes me black and blue. Oh, I hates him. I hates him from me heart."

I can't say the boy's tale was precisely heart-warming, but it gave me a certain thrill of satisfaction, for it meant my plan was back on. "Give me the lantern, boy, and then fetch the horse in a hurry."

He handed over the lantern and dashed for the stable. As he turned the corner, I opened the oil font and splashed it over the wedged chair and door, then shattered the glass and put the wick to the doused material. The flame went up in a blink, and the timbers of the inn were so old and dry that the conflagration spread generally within seconds. As one, a cry of dismay went up from those on the other side of the door.

Now the lad had brought my horse around. I fairly jumped on my mount's back, and held my hand out to the boy. "Climb up behind me!"

He took one look at the rising flames on the front of the inn, heard the panicked shouts and screams from within, and took my hand, hooking his leg over the horse's back. We rode off into the barking cold night.

"'Tis not something I'll blubber over," he said to me after we'd been some minutes in the trees, and were well away from the inn. "But I do wonder where I'll go now. After my mam and pap died, my uncle was all I had."

"I know a Trembler couple," I replied. "They'll take you in. Within a week, you'll never remember you weren't their natural-born son."

He didn't reply, but tightened his arms around me.

"What's your name?" I asked him.

"William, sir, but all call me Willie." A hesitation, and then he asked, "What's your name, sir?"

"My name?" I said. "You're like not to have heard a name like mine before. I'm called Bezaleel."

He did not speak again, his thoughts likely with the rough timbers ablaze miles behind us, as were mine. But if a pang of regret threatened to twinge my heart over the deed, I only had to hearken back to the weight of carrying those heavy chests of my family's fortune to the wagon for Rees the Snook, so many years ago, and then the thought of those flames licking at him seemed to me the sweetest justice.

CALIBAN

I always thought Caliban got short shrift in The Tempest. *I mean, it was his island—Prospera and Miranda were interlopers, and they treat him like a slave! Obviously some unexamined colonialism there. There are hints in the play that Prospero may once have treated him more kindly, but that Caliban repaid him by trying to have his way with Miranda. I try to present how that may have unfolded in this story. I prefer to think of it as expanding on Shakespeare, rather than having the gall to "correct" him.*

This selection appeared in the 2016 Writers of Chantilly anthology, Rewrite the Ending To.... *It actually dates to long before 2016 and is the oldest of the stories in this volume. I originally wrote it in during a summer break in graduate school, although I later revised it heavily for its publication in the anthology.*

The beast clung to the side of the boulder amidst the green slapping waves, muscle-wired legs spread across the rock face like a strand of black algae. With one hand he drove a sharpened stone behind an enrooted mussel, worked it until he wedged out a gap, pried the shell out with his thick nails and dropped it in a little bag hanging from his waist. He'd had good fortune—though little after daybreak, the bag was nearly full.

So engrossed in his task was he, and so unlikely there might be an interruption, that when the shout came he nearly leapt from his perch. The sound had come from out in the bay. Squinting headlong into the spray only gave him an eyeful of saltwater, but clambering higher provided no better view, for the morning fog lay draped heavy across the sea. For an instant the curtain of mist opened, exposing a scene out in the deep water: a vessel, perhaps a figure on its deck. He blinked and the curtain had closed.

No time to waste. In these rock-strewn waters a vessel had

little chance of landing safely. The beast dove, arcing neatly to the waterline. Once in the brine his fluid strokes cut the distance, but the sea was choppy and long minutes passed. No sign of the craft where he had supposed it would be. He treaded water, considering the possibility that it had been an illusion, or already sunk. He swam back and almost at once came upon a wooden hull riding low in the water. A hand reached from the railing to pull him over.

The boat was no more than a glorified raft, a cord-tied bed of rotten planks topped with a leaning cabin for a shelter. A man, rough-shaven, ribs showing, kept his grasp on the beast's hand and leaned towards him, shouting to be heard above the seething sea.

"I thank you for coming to our aid, friend," he said. "I am called Prospero." The man's other arm held a dripping blanket, and in that a pinch-faced child, no more than a toddler. The beast wondered how these two could survive a journey in such a craft.

The man expected a reply, but the beast stared blankly. Eyes flickered, a rusted mind struggled to flip a disused switch. Then a spark caught, and the beast leaned forward and sounded out a response. "Cal—ee—ban." The sounds felt unfamiliar as pebbles in his mouth.

Prospero and Caliban rowed the boat to shore with planks ripped from its cabin. The rising sun burned off the fog and their work soaked them with sweat and sea foam. Though the distance was not far, the currents ran against them and it was late morning before they reached land, dragging the boat through the surf and abandoning it on a bit of sandy shore.

Dazed and dehydrated, Prospero sat and blinked with his child on his knee. Caliban took the man's hands in his, concerned to see the soft flesh torn and bloodied. He probed one of the deepest cuts with his own horny finger and the man angrily withdrew it to his side.

"Do you have water?" Prospero asked him. Another uncomprehending stare. "Waa-ter." Prospero pointed at his mouth.

Caliban gestured for Prospero to rise and follow, led him over the dunes and into the blackwater. At first the man, carrying his child, did not wish to enter the stinking pools, but Caliban pulled at his hand, nodding, a high-pitched snort showing his exasperation. Reluctantly the man waded in after his guide. They passed through mudflats and came to higher ground. Marsh reeds turned to scraggly bush; the wind blew cooler and fresher.

At a steep embankment the beast glided down the grassy incline like an otter, landing in a little stream with hardly a pip, resurfacing to check if the others had followed. The man set his child down, and they gingerly stepped after their host, cupping their hands and drinking greedily at the sweet running water. They drank for a long time, and the man rinsed the blood from his palms and the salt from his beard.

Afterwards Caliban offered his mussels to the man and the child, but Prospero refused to eat them uncooked. Caliban found this odd, since the child whimpered with hunger and the man staggered on his feet. It was long since he'd built a fire, but he recalled the art and let the two rest while he collected grasses and twigs for kindling.

Caliban was eager to please these newcomers to his island and he observed them closely as they sat and ate before the little blaze. They were unlike anything he had seen before. They were made of stuff like him, yet they were different as well: without fur, except on their heads, where their hair grew blonde and fine; and they stood straight when they walked. Their clothes were richly made, though now soiled and ragged.

The man called his child Miranda, and she called him Father, but Caliban had difficulty understanding their words beyond that. His astonishment and curiosity about his visitors only heightened after their meal, when he helped the man unload heavy wooden trunks from the carcass of the grounded boat. He could scarcely wait to discover what they contained.

As the day waned, Caliban took them again to higher ground,

this time to the center of the island where the pine trees grew. There was a place there that might now be useful, a cave that he hid in during storms, though he avoided it at other times because of the strange voices that echoed deep within it. But these two would need the shelter, and besides, he did not think the voices would pester a man such as this.

* * *

The following months were blissful for Caliban. Prospero taught him new words every day, and in turn he performed labors for his new friends. He chopped wood for heat and to build rough furnishings for their cave; he collected mussels, crabs, and roots; he hunted small game; he hauled stones. He showed Prospero all the secrets of the island, not only the location of brooks and streams for fresh water, or which mushrooms could be eaten without becoming sick, but also all the gloomy places in the marsh and the woods where he sometimes heard disembodied groans and murmurs. It was these last that most interested Prospero.

As the months passed, Prospero had less and less time for Caliban. The contents of the trunks had proved not so interesting—only musty old books. Yet Prospero spent hours every day poring over them and reciting in strange languages. And whenever Caliban showed him some new hidden spot where he had encountered an invisible spirit or a floating light that moved of its own accord, it would propel Prospero back to his tomes for more study.

Despite the multitude of tasks Prospero had for him, he did not work Caliban onerously. During his free time, Caliban played with Miranda. He adored the little girl, accompanying her everywhere as she toddled about on her plump little legs. She was infinitely curious about every aspect of the island, and Caliban was eager to satisfy. Though Prospero did not allow her to wander too far into the dangerous wilderness, Caliban had many wonderful things to show her near the cave.

Her favorite activity was gathering the marsh mallow flowers with Caliban, which he collected and boiled in a clay pot, skimming off the white film that rose to the surface with a branch. When it cooled they shared the sweet goo, pulling it away from the stick with their teeth. On trips to the beach, these supervised by Prospero, he showed her the way to catch hermit crabs as they dug themselves in after a wave receded, and where to find the black triangular teeth that had once dwelt in the mouth of a shark.

Miranda in turn adored Caliban. When he laid himself on the ground she picked burrs from his long hair and scratched his back. They understood each other, talked at the same level, and Caliban answered her many questions about the world in a more satisfactory way than her father did. "What is that smell?" she might ask Caliban, wrinkling her nose, as they walked along the shore.

"That? Is smell of grass, after dead," he would respond, and demonstrate how to break off the end of the cordgrass to suck out its salty juice. Much more sensible than her father's response to the same question: "That, my dear, is the stench of *Spartina patens* in a state of decay."

Caliban was happy now, and it did not take him long to forget his life before the arrival of Prospero and Miranda. When he tried to remember, it seemed odd, like the life of another person. He had lived alone for many seasons. He had not been lonely exactly, for he had not known about friendship, yet he had often felt a yearning that was something like loneliness. And before that time, he had lived with his dam, Sycorax.

Indeed, Sycorax's death was one memory that came to him involuntarily and with regularity. Of the old crone herself he recalled little, and that mostly unpleasant—she had been harsh and ugly and had often thrashed him viciously—but the morning he found her body, still and rigid, burned sharp in his memory even now. Her eyes wide open, the crazy evil faded from them but still entirely blue, so that Caliban had not been sure she was really dead until he closed the lids with his own fingers. He had decided that she might return to haunt him if he left the body out, so he dragged it to the marsh where it bubbled down into the black water. He gathered her books and scrolls from the cave, her home then even as it was Prospero's and Miranda's home now. It was the last time for a long while he visited the cave without fear.

Confusion and hunger followed the weeks after her death. Although he had fended for himself in most things as long as he could remember, he had still depended on Sycorax for a sorry sort of companionship and some meat. Not until he worked out the tricks for catching rabbits and marmosets could he feed himself adequately. At dusk he lit fires and burned her books, amused by the phosphorescent letters, funny voices, and moving pictures that drifted out of the fire along with the smoke.

When he had burned the last book and learned to feed himself well enough that his belly did not hurt when he laid down to sleep, Caliban achieved a sort of peace. He gradually came to understand that he was the owner of the island, and its king. And so he had lived for unknowable years before this new phase of his life.

* * *

The island had always hinted at its otherworldly secrets. At night, pained moans emanated from the deep hidden places, and the breezes carried whispers in languages familiar and strange. Sometimes during the drowsy afternoons, when Caliban climbed a bald cypress and lay cradled in the high branches, he could hear singing in the far distance as he teetered between sleep and wake, though whether the ethereal harmonies were real or only dreams he never was sure.

But since the arrival of the visitors the spirits had dropped their shyness, parading luminously through the pine forest after sunset, or rushing invisibly through the crowns of trees even during the day. Perhaps Prospero and Miranda had displaced the spirits by moving into the cave, Caliban mused, or maybe their arrival had simply excited the attention of the island's supernatural residents. It was not until one evening after the weather turned cool that Caliban realized Prospero himself was actually calling the apparitions.

On this night the wind lashed like a whip: one of the storms that periodically overtook the island in late summer or early fall. Caliban had settled into his mossy nest but the weather kept him awake, so he just laid and stared into the night sky, inky with dark clouds. After a while he heard footsteps passing underneath. He peered down through the branches and was amazed to see Prospero approaching, led by three tiny, glowing wisps. The man strode through the wood with purpose, his face determined below his silver hair, a gust billowing his robes up behind him in flapping lengths of cloth.

When he had passed, Caliban slunk down and followed at a distance. They wound their way through ever denser underbrush and into marshy terrain. Soon they were wading through mud, Prospero apparently unconcerned that his fine robes might be ruined. It reminded Caliban of the first day his guests had arrived, only this time it was Prospero leading him.

Now they entered the deepest marsh, their three glowing guides the only source of light in the humid gloom. They stopped at a patch of dry ground where a huge cloven loblolly pine grew. It was a tree Caliban knew well, and detested. Its gnarled old bark seemed to take the form of a sobbing face, its twisted branches stretched askew like broken limbs, crimson sap dripped from scores in its trunk. On this night, the winds high in its branches shrieked like a wounded animal.

Prospero stepped up onto the little patch of raised earth, his robes dry and clean, his glowing guides circling him in a slow orbit. The old pine's shrieking grew louder still, as if it were the tree itself responding to the approaching visitor.

Prospero raised his arms and shouted: "Silence!"

The wind ceased. The whole swamp fell silent as a stone.

Prospero laid his right hand on the tree's trunk. "Open!" he cried, and a cleft in the trunk yawned wide. A pale arm tentatively reached out, and Prospero grabbed it and began to pull. Soon there was a shoulder, a torso, and with a final jerk Prospero yanked a whole body from the tree, the two of them tumbling to the ground. The body had the shape of a woman, unclothed, long-haired, scrawny-limbed, marble white skin streaked with dark sap or maybe blood.

The figure pulled herself to her knees and bowed her head before Prospero. "My savior!" she sang out trembling high. "For twelve years I have been imprisoned in this pine, stretched and squeezed and torn. For twelve years I have howled, and no one has heard my cries."

Prospero had recovered his feet and straightened himself to his full height. "Speak your name, spirit."

"I am Ariel."

"And I am Prospero. Inform me who it was imprisoned you in this tree?"

"It was the witch Sycorax, a most terrible and—"

"So I thought," Prospero said, cutting her off. "I have freed you from your torment, Ariel, but not out of sympathy. At a time to come, I will have need of your aids, and you shall serve me or I will shut you up again. Only after you have performed for me truly will I release you. Do you accept this offer?"

Ariel flung herself to the ground at Prospero's feet. "Yes, master, whatever you wish. Only tell me what to do!"

"Your service shall not begin yet. It may be tomorrow, or a year from now. You may fly free, but you must not leave this island. Keep your ear to the wind, and when on some future day you hear me call your name, you shall return and pay your debt to me. Do you understand what I have spoken?"

"Every word, master."

"Very well. You are free now until I call you."

With this, Prospero spun and stepped back into the marsh, his glowing guides leading the way. He came to the clump of grasses where Caliban had hidden himself and stopped short. Caliban's heart jumped and he held his breath. He was not sure why he was afraid, but felt he had witnessed something he should not have. Prospero only smiled to himself a moment and continued on his way.

Back in his nest, Caliban reflected long into the night. Prospero's mastery of the island's spirits surpassed even Sycorax's, and he felt honored he should have chosen this island to rule, out of all the places in the world he might have picked. Yet Caliban questioned the wisdom of releasing Ariel. Though he had been only a small creature, he recalled that his dam had once employed Ariel as well, but had shut her up in the tree for disobedience and mischief. With a troubled mind he fell into fitful sleep.

He awoke suddenly in the darkest, coldest part of the night, sure he had heard a noise close at hand. Fright stabbed his gut and he slowly turned his head side to side. There was nothing but blackness. The earlier wind had retreated and all was still. Out of the corner of his eye he thought he caught a spark and he flipped his head around, but there was nothing. Probably only a trick of his own mind. Caliban calmed his ragged breathing and forced himself to sit up.

Before he could, unseen hands grabbed him from behind and snatched him from the nest. He had the sickening sensation of falling and tumbled through the tree branches, thumping and bouncing to the ground where he lay in a mass of bruises. Someone pulled a sack of gauzy material over his face and pushed his head down. Malicious giggles and cackles and echoes surrounded him. The one holding the sack giggled loudest of all.

Caliban struggled to wriggle free but the hands held him firm. Something pricked his skin, a tiny heated pinch. He howled and yelped, and the voices shouted with glee to hear him. Then there was another and another, and the cumulative effect mounted until he doubled over under a scalding shower of pain. He held his arms tight at his sides and rolled over to protect his tender middle, but the pinches sent searing little tracks of white-hot intensity burrowing into his folded flesh. One giggling voice sang a mocking little tune:

Caliban, of Sycorax issued,
hag whose dark spells
the goodly spirits misused,
her son in the tree limbs dwells.
We shall visit thee nightly!
Teach thee most sprightly!
And you will dream of Ariel!

Caliban whined and sobbed, fueling the amusement of his tormentors. The laughing and pinching grew, until he felt as if they gouged out little chunks of his flesh with each prick. He was sure he would soon expire.

"Stop!" A booming voice full of command, and all action came to an instant halt. "Release him."

Somebody lifted the sack from Caliban's head. Ariel floated above him, now attired in some shimmering dress, glowing softly. She held the sack in one hand. All around a cascade of tiny, winged sparks bobbed and flitted in the air.

The voice was Prospero's, who now stepped into view. "Why do you torment this beast, Ariel?"

"But master, this whelpling is the son of she who imprisoned me," Ariel sang out.

"This creature does not carry the sins of his mother. He is in my care and you will not harm him."

"Oh, sir, we did not harm. You will see there is not a mark on his body nor a hair plucked from his head. It was but a game we played."

Ariel covered her face with her arm, but Prospero grabbed her wrist and looked her in the eye. "Hear me, spirit! You shall not beleaguer this creature. Leave him be! Now quit this place, and disturb my servant no more."

He released his grip and Ariel flew off in a rush above the treetops, followed by a glimmering trail of tiny winged sparks. Prospero stooped to gather up Caliban in his arms. He carried him to his cave and wrapped him in a blanket, holding him until he stopped shivering. He laid him at the foot of his bed, where Caliban, feeling for the first time truly safe and loved, slept sounder than he ever had.

* * *

Years swam by like fishes in a lake, so slippery and elusive that Caliban hardly noticed their passage. He dressed now like his friends, but felt always constrained by his clothes. He ate his meals with them, though still preferred his mussels raw. He and Miranda were constant companions, and as she grew she surpassed him in understanding. Prospero continued to teach them both, but where Caliban still stumbled over reading the simplest lessons, Miranda had begun to read the Latin and Greek works of antiquity; still, their fondness for each other ran deep. It was not in Caliban's nature to ponder the future, but if he had, he would have pictured it with Miranda by his side forever.

It happened one year during that mild season when the world becomes drowsy in the mid-afternoon sun. Caliban lurked in the cooler shadows of the foliage at the top of an embankment, absentmindedly gnawing open the brown burred balls from a sweet gum tree and probing his tongue inside the cracked half to tease out the seeds. His eyes were trained on the stream below, where Miranda bathed. It was her favorite spot for soaking, a shoulder-deep pool at the foot of a miniature waterfall where the rushing water foamed. She washed her body without shame, unaware he watched. She probably would not have felt shame before Caliban in any case.

Caliban observed her figure. As she had grown, she had taken the shape of his dam, only more so: smoother skin, longer legs, fleshier breasts, wider hips. He had lately become fascinated with

Miranda's body, and often hid here to watch her undress. He recalled how previously they had frolicked together at this place, splashing and chasing one another through the water, dribbling sand between their fingers to build delicate castles on the bank. Caliban did not join her to play in the stream anymore, however, for he was afraid of the fervor that now colored his feelings towards her.

On this day she was lovelier than ever. Her skin was summer-brown and after washing she submerged herself, swimming across the pool in graceful strokes, breaking the surface long enough to take ravenous breaths and shake sparkling drops from her flowing hair. After a while she waded into the shallower water at one end of the pool and ran her hands over her face. Caliban's breathing grew rapid and shallow and he reached with one hand to rub the swelling that had formed under his breeches. Gathering his courage, he called out, "Miranda!"

She turned with a little look of surprise that melted into a smile. "Caliban! I didn't know you were there."

"I came here to swim. It is so hot today."

"Come down here. We haven't swum together for so long!" She slipped again beneath the water.

Caliban stripped off his clothes and slid down into the water himself. He was a strong and fast swimmer, and glided beneath the water like an eel. He chased Miranda, grabbed her foot and wiggled his finger across it. Miranda shot towards the surface and splashed at him with a giggling exhalation.

"Stop it, that tickles!"

"Are you sure it wasn't a fish?" Caliban teased.

"No, it was you. Ooh, look, my skin is almost as brown as yours," she said, holding her sunned arm up to his. "By the end of the summer we'll be twins."

Caliban looked at his own black, hairy skin and smiled, flattered by her comment. He reached out to touch her arm again, but she was off, and he after her, playing their not-yet-forgotten childhood game, the shark and the minnow. They alternated roles with each turn: he the hunter, she the prey; and then reversed. Of course he always caught her quickly when it was his turn as the shark. Even when he gave her a head start it wouldn't be long until his hand brushed her foot, her arm, her hair, and the turn would end. And he let her catch him when she was the pursuer. After one round, he was surprised when she caught his foot, and with her other hand grabbed his calf, and as they rose to the surface together she embraced him from behind.

Her soft breast pressed against him and the underwater eddies from the kicking of her legs tickled his skin. He wriggled free of her embrace and dove down, coming up behind her, letting his fingers trace over her body as he rose. He pulled her to a shallow part of the pool, now guiding his hands over her, and he pressed himself against her thigh. Miranda let out a breath with an undertone like a purr, and Caliban maneuvered himself to join with her in union. He understood now all the strange fitful dreams he had dreamt lately—they had meant this, only this was real, and he knew it to be the culmination of his love for Miranda. But then, just as in his dreams, it was broken off.

A hand grabbed his shoulder, and Caliban found himself swiveled roughly around and staring straight into Prospero's crimson face. They stood in ankle-deep water, and Caliban felt ashamed of his nakedness without knowing why. Prospero shoved him onto the sand and knocked him to the ground with a fist heavier than Caliban would have thought possible from an old man. Miranda shrieked to no avail as Prospero lifted Caliban up by his hair.

"You!" he sputtered. "You, whom we raised like a very member of our family, and this is how you repay us—by endeavoring to take the honor of my child! I was a fool to believe a beast like you capable of anything but evil."

Caliban tried to stammer a reply, an apology, anything, but his mouth was thick and unable to form the words. Prospero cast him again to the ground.

"Hear my pronouncement, brute. No longer are you under

my protection, and you may no longer enter our dwelling. If ever I find you alone with my daughter again, it will be at the cost of your life."

Caliban scrambled to his feet and fled into the trees, forgetting his clothes.

* * *

"Caliban! Caliban!"

Caliban lifted his head from his arms and gazed into the night's darkness, unable to identify the source of the whispers.

"Behind you, silly," came the giggling voice, and Caliban turned his head to see a dim glowing. His eyes took in the silhouette and he recognized Ariel's shape. Alarm gripped him.

"What do you want with me?" he asked.

Ariel tittered and began to sing:

Caliban the Bastard-King
knew the secrets of his isle
he wished to make Miranda queen
but Ariel outwitted him with her guile.
She paid a visit to a father
and informed him better of his daughter
and Caliban lost his queen!

Caliban swiveled around and clutched at Ariel but she darted out of his grasp. Behind her the air began to buzz and glow with hundreds of winged sparks. It dawned on Caliban what it might mean to sleep outside the cave without Prospero's protection. He curled into a ball to protect his tender parts, knowing it would do no good.

* * *

Their revels now were ended, the guests aboard their ships and bound for Naples. The spirits too, seemed melted into thin air, for now no unseen instruments played for the moon or on distant winds, and the sun shone over the island with perfect tranquility. Only Caliban remained.

For days, he roamed the isle, trying to put out of his head the images of Miranda and Fernando, playing chess together, walking together, laughing together, holding hands or giving the other a gentle kiss on the forehead. The celebration had been joyous but Caliban had not taken part, embarrassed and preferring to assuage his guilty conscience through labor for Prospero. But now, his exertions over, he was not even sure what his guilt had been for.

It occurred to him one day to explore the abandoned cave. With the spirits departed there was no need for him to fear it, so he lit a long branch for light and entered. The rough-hewn wooden furniture remained behind. Caliban could use it as firewood, or perhaps even to build a rude dwelling for himself. The trunks of clothes and personal effects were gone, as expected.

He advanced farther, into the deep hidden chambers he had never been permitted to see. On entering these, he drew in his breath in whistling surprise. Prospero had left behind all the arts of his magic: the heavy robes, dusty books, golden bands and engraved wands, writing tools and ingenious little mechanical devices.

Caliban gathered all of these things and carried them in bundles to the long field where Prospero had so often practiced his conjuring. Night was imminent when Caliban had finished. He realized he lacked one thing still: a throne like the one Prospero had sat in.

The next morning he began to chop apart the furniture and refashion the lumber into a replica of Prospero's strange seat. He built it precisely as he remembered it, down to the attached panel where he impressed jewels of various colors to replace the blinking and flashing lights. After a few days, he judged his work satisfactory, and proceeded with the next step.

Caliban vested himself in one of the magic robes and opened a book, examining its long lists of words and numbers. He placed Prospero's funny crown on his head, the one he had seen him wear so many times, pulling the odd little flaps over his ears and carefully positioning the jutting stick in front of his mouth. Finally, he took one of the wands in his hands. After fumbling with the etchings and bumps on its surface, he worked out how to slide a piece of its base into a certain position, causing the tips to glow green and white.

Caliban waited impatiently for nightfall. He was eager to try out his control over the supernatural, fantasizing about what such power could do for him. Never again would he have to scale rocks collecting mussels, or chop wood, or chase the island's brown rabbits until they tired and lay panting for him to grab by the ears. One of Prospero's spirits could finish the job in moments; maybe he could even summon Ariel herself. What pleasure it would be, seeing her sweat through a hard day's labor while he enjoyed himself in leisure!

Finally the sun set red, last light dripping from the sky like blood from a hung carcass. Caliban began his imitation of the routine he had secretly watched Prospero perform so many times. He mumbled names and numbers into the jutting stick. He paraded up and down the field, waving the glowing wands. He made motions with his hands over the bejeweled panel. When nothing happened, he repeated it again, precisely as he recalled Prospero doing. Still nothing. He tried again, and again, varying his actions just slightly, changing the incantations, adjusting his motions, his posture, the volume of his voice, but still no spirits came, their great glowing bodies lighting the field like the noonday sun, the hot roar of their breath blowing poisonous vapors into the air. He knew the problem must be that he was not reciting the right words, for the language in the books was strange. He would just have to repeat the contents until he stumbled across the proper syllables to make the magic work.

Dawn broke, and no spirits had been conjured. Caliban's throat ached raw and tight from speaking all night. Yet he was not beaten. He would have to try again the next night. Maybe spirits only came on certain nights, or when the moon held a certain shape. Prospero had used knowledge Caliban did not have, so he would have to persevere.

But no spirits came that night, nor the next, nor any night after, no matter the shape of the moon or the level of the tide or the weather. After weeks, Caliban had to admit to himself that the secret to conjuring was not contained in the magic robes, the crown with the ear flaps, the glowing rod (although that did prove useful for lighting his way at night), or any other of Prospero's books or tools. At dawn one overcast morning he finally gave up, throwing down the wizardly accoutrements.

He swam out to a rock jutting from the sea, sat on the top pondering gloomily as the waves wetted his feet. He remembered this was, in fact, the same rock where he had been collecting mussels the morning Miranda and Prospero had first appeared on their ragged little boat. But now they were gone and the island belonged to him again. He could do as he pleased, with no one to stop him. Why was that thought no comfort?

Caliban gazed into the fog and realized he was afraid. Before he had feared the night, the cave, the spirits, the dark places in the marsh. But those no longer held any anxiety for him; his fear now was different. It was not the anticipation of pain or hunger. It was a fear of being alone. More than that, it was the knowledge that there would be no respite from this condition. He would never again have companionship.

There was only one thing to do now: return to his island and crown himself king. He dove off the rock and swam for shore.

A FAR OCEAN'S TALE

This story gives us a glimpse into the past of one of Mother Ink's *most popular supporting characters, Gray-Patch the telepathic ray. This story actually preceded my writing of the Last Days of Atlantis by many years. Back in 2007-09, I wrote my first novel, a science-fiction middle grade book which was terrible and will never see the light of day. But there was one character in it who I couldn't forget, and that was Gray-Patch. I cut out the place in that novel where she explains her background to the other characters and greatly expanded it for this story. Later, when I started writing The Last Days of Atlantis series in 2019, I decided she had a place in that world and re-used her. Despite its age, this story has never been seen in print before.*

Gray-Patch peered over the edge of the Big Well, but could see nothing but blackness. No one knew what lay at the bottom. Only one other had ever gone all the way down and returned.

She looked over at Swift and the others. They watched her expectantly. She could feel the anticipation buzzing in their minds. The Big Well lay beyond the canyon, where the young rays weren't supposed to go. Even to be here was risking punishment, never mind the danger of what she was about to do.

"You first or me?" Swift mind-flashed her.

Best to get it over with. "Me." She hesitated a moment on the edge to steel her will for the ordeal and dove into the rocky maw.

As she spiraled down deeper and deeper, the light went from green to blue to violet, the temperature from cool to chilly to ice-cold. Finally, the light faded out altogether and Gray-Patch swam down in darkness. The pressure grew so great it pained her skull. But she had to keep going. She wondered how far down she was, but the inky blackness provided no way to gauge the depth.

Numbness slowly spread from the tips of her wings, whether from the temperature or the pressure Gray-Patch did not know. Her head felt almost as if it would pop. She could not bear it much longer. Finally, she hit cold, slimy mud. She curled the prehensile tip of her wing to scoop up a glob of it and turned towards the surface. The return trip went quickly as she ascended into warmth, light, and color.

She emerged from the Big Well and the other rays gathered around her. Had she really done it? She flung the mud from her wing, sending the glob spinning through the water, black and glistening. Not a word was mind-flashed, but she could perceive their astonishment.

Gray-Patch felt exultation rise inside her. In their youthful memories, only one other had ever reached the bottom: Surestroke. Surestroke, her brother, whom she had not seen since he had gone away to the Great City so months ago.

Swift pushed the other rays aside and swam to the edge. "My turn."

"It's really bad down there," Gray-Patch said. "You don't have to do it if you don't want to."

Swift looked at her with disgust. She could sense his mood, a little nervous, but mostly an angry determination not to be shown up by a mere female. No sense trying to change his mind now.

Swift dove down and Gray-Patch joined the others in watching him plunge down until he was only a speck in the deep murk, before disappearing altogether.

The rays joked and wrestled with one another while they waited. But many minutes passed and the little speck did not reappear, and the group grew serious and tense. "Shouldn't he be back by now?" someone mind-flashed. "Do you think he's okay?" "Maybe we should go look for him."

The other rays turned to Gray-Patch. "You've been to the bottom. You should go find him." Gray-Patch had no desire to go back down into the cold blackness, but it was true the responsibility fell on her.

"Maybe he'll show up in a few minutes. He's probably taking his time, teasing us." But Gray-Patch knew that wasn't true.

Finally, too much time had passed to deny he must be in trouble. Gray-Patch dove down, broadcasting Swift's name as far and as loudly as she could muster, but even after she pushed herself to the bottom and touched the cold mud again, she received no answer. She came back to the surface, hoping Swift had turned up while she was gone. He had not.

When the sun set that night, the search party had to give up. No one was willing to admit it, but the truth was obvious: Swift was gone. Even the adult rays found the conditions at the bottom of the Big Well excruciating. A young ray could not possibly survive such cold and pressure for the hours Swift had been missing.

Gray-Patch and her parents returned very late to her family's balmy, protected lagoon. She was exhausted yet unable to sleep, and simply swam around the lagoon in restless circles.

"Having trouble sleeping, my little pup?" her father mind-flashed.

"I keep remembering what happened, over and over," she said. "If I had done things differently, this wouldn't have happened."

"My darling pup, this was not your fault," her mother said, but Gray-Patch thought she detected some doubt.

And after all, it was her fault. So many things she could have changed. If she hadn't accepted Swift's challenge in the first place, if she hadn't gone out past the ridge, if she had gone down to search for him earlier....

It was the middle of the night when she sensed presences outside their lagoon. Her parents were asleep, so she floated discreetly into the little channel that led outside. Two rays were just beyond it. Grown-ups.

"Stop, please don't do this!" She recognized the mind-flash as Swift's mother. "You are enraged, you do not know what you're doing!"

"I don't care! Stop blocking my way, female!" It was Swift's father. "I'm going to demand justice be brought for that little sea snake!"

"Please, stop! She's young, she didn't mean for anything to happen."

"I don't care if she isn't grown -- our son was a pup too! If it wasn't for her, goading him into that stupid dive. I always knew she was dangerous, she and that brother of hers."

"You're right, my dear mate. But it's the wrong time. We can't just charge into their lagoon in the night. In the morning we'll bring up the matter of justice with the Elders."

Gray-Patch slowly backstroked, keeping her mind blank so Swift's parents wouldn't notice her. Back in the lagoon, she swam around furiously, trying to work out her options. Clearly, she could not remain. Justice? For a murder, that would mean at the very least exile, but likelier even death. A death for a death, that's what the Elders would say.

Better for her to leave now and not drag her parents into this.

The next morning, Gray-Patch was already far from the cozy, intricate network of lagoons and shallows that she had known her entire life, past the canyon that until now had marked the boundary of her world. She had entered the Sea Forest, of which she had heard much but never seen.

The giant kelp of the forest floated thickly on top of the water, their roots dangling down for hundreds of feet. The water here was suffused with a wan, yellowish-green light. Any number of lurking menaces could take cover in the dim light and abundant growth, and because the entanglements of roots hindered her progress, the going was slow. But she was lucky enough to avoid danger and reached the forest's end by midday.

In the afternoon she sped across the expanses of the Barrens, a vast, undersea desert. Swimming here was easy for no obstructions rose before her and swift currents were at her tail, but the danger was no less than before. In the Barrens, nothing grew or lived, for to let even a single poisonous grain of sand pass into the gills meant certain death. She dared not stop, even for a moment.

Finally, as evening fell, Gray-Patch reached a long ridge, riddled with caves. Such a place was likely inhabited, but no telling if the locals were friendly. She cautiously approached a rocky outcropping and sent out a general mind-tap: "Is it possible for a traveler to find shelter in this place?"

An ancient ray, mottled and frail, emerged from a cleft and looked her over. "Headed to the Great City, are ye?" he asked in an archaic dialect.

"Yes, how do you know that?"

The old ray laughed. "No other reason for a wee niblin like ye to stop here now, is there? This must be ye first visit to the City. Ye never forget the first visit." He gave her a wink.

"Yes, but I do not travel for pleasure."

"Oh, the niblin be in some trouble, then? Such a shame. But no matter, I think I have a place for ye ready all the same." The old ray escorted her to a cave, its interior plain but clean.

Despite her fatigue from the day's long swim, Gray-Patch could hardly sleep that night. Her memories of the family and life she left behind and thoughts of her coming reunion with her brother, Surestroke, occupied her mind until long after darkness had fallen.

In the morning, she set out again. The ridge opened out onto a giant reef extending past the horizon, every inch of it teeming with fish of all colors and sizes. She had never seen such a variety and quantity of life. Aware that she was drawing nearer to her destination, Gray-Patch relaxed and set a more leisurely pace so she could take her time looking around her surroundings. As she swam on, she passed an increasing number of rays harvesting oysters, clams, and snails, no doubt for the feeding of the Great

City's residents.

Around midday, she spotted in the distance great gray walls rising hundreds of feet, from the ocean floor up to where the water met the empty world of air above. This was it: the Great City, the metropolis of which so many tales were told.

Soon she arrived at the outer walls. A pair of massive gates was open for the day, but before Gray-Patch could pass through, a huge ray swam up to her. His wings were scarred and embedded with shells -- the marks of a warrior of the City Guard.

"What is your business?" he asked.

"I am a traveler from the Southern Lagoons and here to visit my brother."

"And who is your brother?"

"His name is Surestroke. He left us months ago to join the City Guard."

"Ah, Surestroke! I know the fellow. One of our brightest recruits. It is a pleasure to meet you. But if I may ask, why does a young female travel alone on such a dangerous journey?"

Gray-Patch thought it best not to explain too much. "I carry bad news from home. But I would rather not speak of it."

"Of course, your business is your own. You may proceed. You will find Surestroke at the barracks in the center of the city." He mind-flashed her a series of landmarks she would see to know she was headed the right way and gestured for her to proceed through the gates.

Gray-Patch's first impression of the City was of the crowds of rays, thousands upon thousands swimming in every direction at once. Everybody seemed so busy and focused. She felt acutely how plain she must look to these sophisticated city dwellers.

She passed through crammed residential passages, squalid and dim, and soared along broad commercial avenues between towering columns, massive ziggurats, and imposing gates. Everywhere she looked, all was made of carved stone or shaped coral and every surface draped in exotic plants, urchins, and anemones gathered from all over the ocean.

After some time, she found a giant tower near the center of the city. Its entire surface was painted with friezes of armies of rays defeating the Great City's dangerous enemies: ravenous giant serpents; toothy, vicious saw-lizards; and most menacing of all, five-legged barbarian pentapi, war-like cousins to the gentle octopus. This must be the barracks.

Gray-Patch explained herself to a guard at an entrance who promptly went off to find her brother. In a few minutes he returned, Surestroke behind him.

Surestroke glided over to greet her with a rub of his nose against hers. "Gray-Patch! I am so glad to see you! But what are you doing here?"

She returned her brother's greeting and explained the situation. His demeanor turned from joyous to worried. "This is a serious matter indeed, sister. Let us go for a swim and mind-flash of what we can do."

Along some of the City's less crowded byways they talked. "I do not believe you committed murder, sister. It was not your fault this happened."

"And yet it seems I must face justice nevertheless. It will be easier for our mother and father if I never go back."

"Perhaps." Surestroke did not speak for a long while.

Gray-Patch broke the silence. "What is that you are wearing?" she asked him, pointing to the large, crenellated white shells embedded in the center of each of his wings.

"Ah, yes, these," Surestroke said with some self-importance. "The sign of a recruit. Every new shell I get shows an increase in rank or marks my participation in a great battle. These are the first of many shells to come, I hope!"

"Didn't it hurt to have them put on?" Gray-Patch asked.

"Yes, but what does pain mean to a warrior like me? A small price to pay for the honor of serving in the City Guard!"

Gray-Patch felt proud of her brother, but tinged with worry for the dangers that awaited him. She had already lost her home and her parents. Would her brother be next?

Before the end of the day, Surestroke located a grotto in an unfashionable quarter where Gray-Patch could live in an unoccupied cave. It wasn't much, but it also wasn't too far from the barracks, so it would be easy for Surestroke to check on her.

Just as they were about to part, Surestroke spotted a group of fellow recruits. He greeted them and introduced his sister. Some of the recruits were good friends and he fell into a spirited conversation.

Gray-Patch noticed one of the other recruits in particular. Broadwing was his name, and his name suited him, for his wings were wide and muscular, though his face was set with gentle brown eyes. He must have noticed Gray-Patch as well, for he did not remove his gaze from her the entire time they were near.

Gray-Patch said good-bye to her brother and took her leave from the rest of the group, begging her exhaustion after a long day. As she turned to go, Broadwing sent a gentle mind-tap to her, so subtle no one else in the group noticed, a sort of light kiss just for her. Her face and wings grew warm with embarrassment.

Gray-Patch returned to her grotto but could not get her mind off the handsome recruit she had met. She decided to return to the barracks later that night to see him again.

She waited until long after darkness had fallen and the city calmed down before venturing out of the cave. The passages and boulevards were lit at night by swarms of small, phosphorescent fishes. Truly, the wonders and conveniences of the Great City were endless! With the light from the fishes, it was no trouble for her to find her way back, where she approached the first guard she saw. Too nervous to speak, she simply mind-flashed the guard an image of Broadwing. The guard went in and a few minutes later, Broadwing appeared.

"Gray-Patch!" Broadwing stammered a bit over his next words. "I was hoping to find a way for us to meet in private, but I did not dare to think it would be so soon."

"I knew that I had to meet you again, no matter what

happened," Gray-Patch said. "I didn't think I could survive if I didn't see you before dawn."

"I feel the same way. Alas, I am not supposed to be out of the barracks after dark, and must return soon so the sergeant doesn't notice my absence!"

"A few minutes is enough, so long as I know you share my feelings."

"Yes, I do. And I still can't believe you really came! Truly, your audacity is matched only by your beauty!"

Gray-Patch found herself flustered by the compliment, but no response was necessary as Broadwing gently ran the tip of his wing across her face. The intimate gesture stirred unfamiliar feelings inside her.

Their time together ended all too quickly but even so Gray-Patch knew by the end of it she was in love with Broadwing, and he with her. And so it went every night for weeks, the two sneaking moments together whenever Broadwing could slip away, gliding along the avenues together, or taking a quick visit to one of the cleaning stations where armies of angelfish, butterflyfish, and half a dozen other species waited to nibble away the dead skin or little worms from the rays' bodies. So much faster and more thorough than the tiny cleaning station back at the Southern Lagoons!

Yet despite the delights of the Great City, the days felt endless to her, while the time with her beloved was as precious as the rarest conch shell.

The day came when Surestroke and Broadwing finished their training. Gray-Patch attended the shell-embedding ceremony and afterwards she joined her brother on a celebratory swim around the monuments and huge public spaces of the city.

"So will you and Broadwing come with me to the lagoon?" Surestroke asked.

"Whatever for?" Gray-stroke said.

"To wed, of course."

Gray-Stroke was mute. They had been so discreet, or so she had thought!

"Your silence betrays you," Surestroke said. "But I have known since the first day you two met. I saw how you looked at each other. And I noted Broadwing's absence every evening, leaving after the sergeant had departed."

Gray-Patch laughed. "You have caught me, brother! But you know returning home is impossible. Even if our own parents are over the shame of what I did, how could the others ever forgive me?"

Surestroke considered. "Then you two must wed here. Tomorrow will be the day."

"So soon?"

"Why wait any longer? I will make all the arrangements. Let us go find Broadwing so you two can go off and enjoy yourselves." Surestroke and Gray-Patch soon found Broadwing near the barracks and the two lovers went off together. They quickly found a private spot in a coral park where they could nuzzle together without interruption.

Life with Broadwing proved idyllic for Gray-Patch. They moved from her grotto cave to a more fitting dwelling in one of the large towers in the city's center. It was not long before Gray-Patch gave birth to twins, a boy and a girl. The two took great joy in watching their two little pups grow up, year after year.

One season, the tides ran cold, a bad omen. Sure enough, it wasn't long before an army of pentapi rode the cold current from a distant sea, arriving in the reef outside the Great City and staging a series of attacks against outlying communities.

The City Guard was engaged day and night in battles. Gray-Patch feared for the safety of her mate and her brother, and the tales that Broadwing brought home did little to assuage her worry. He mind-flashed images of the battles against the cunning, five-legged pentapi, who kidnapped the rays as slaves to haul loads for their marauding armies as they traveled the oceans.

One day, a member of the City Guard Gray-Patch had never seen arrived at their home. She knew before a word was exchanged that something terrible had happened.

"Are you Gray-Patch, mate of Broadwing?" he asked.

"I am."

"It is my sad duty to inform you that Broadwing has been injured in battle. His injuries are life-threatening and we dare not move him, but if you hurry, we may be able to reach him while he is still alive."

Gray-Patch left her pups in the care of a friendly neighbor, giving them a final nuzzle before setting off. The other ray led the way outside the city to a strangely empty area of the reef, as if all the normal inhabitants had fled. The only sign of life were the dozens of casualties from the day's battle, sunk to the bottom, torn and bloodied, sending out desperate, painful mind-flashes in their death throes. Broadwing was among them. Surestroke, unharmed, was by his side.

Gray-Patch swam to her mate and brother. "You've come," Broadwing said to her, but his mind-flash was weak.

"Shush, don't speak," she said. "Conserve your strength." She did her best to comfort him, flashing him images of their pups, healthy and happy, and memories of their own joyful times together. Surestroke maintained a respectful distance. After a few minutes, the mind-connection between Gray-Patch and Broadwing ended. He was gone. Gray-Patch hovered over his body for long minutes, hardly aware of the world around her.

She wasn't sure when it started, but after a while she became aware of a commotion nearby. She looked up and saw the battle had restarted. A band of a dozen or more pentapi passed above her, a sight more awful than she had imagined. Their faces had beady red eyes and curved beaks, their bodies were clad in a sort of shell armor, and their tentacles clutched jagged spears.

Surestroke moved over her, covering her protectively. Black ink clouded the water and she could not see. She sensed

Surestroke thrashing above her and then his body was gone. From out of nowhere, a pentapus appeared directly in front of her, striking her on the head with his spear before she could dodge him. Slowly, she sank down, watching a little cloud of blood spread through the water above her. It occurred to her the blood must be her own.

The world faded slowly out. Her thoughts drifted back to her youth and the lagoon she had not seen for so long, and then to the day of that horrible accident years before. It struck her now that despite her hasty assumption at the time, of course she would not have been punished for Swift's accidental death. How foolish she had been to leave and never return!

Knowing her love for her own pups, she realized her parents must have missed her terribly all this time. Not knowing what had become of her had surely been a burden for them as they aged. Gray-Patch had a pang of regret her mother and father had never even seen their grandchildren. And that was the last thing she thought of before everything went black.

When Gray-Patch came to she found the reef eerie and desolate, the dark waters empty of movement or mind-flashes. For a long time she dared not move. What if those evil creatures were still out there? But she could not lie still forever.

She ventured to advance a little. Nothing. She swam low and vigilant just above the reef surface, ready to dive into a crevice at any sign of danger. But there was no one and nothing until she reached the Great City. To her astonishment and horror, she found no guards at the great gates, which were wide open even now, when it must be late into the night.

In the city itself, the inhabitants had fled the streets and closed up their homes. Many buildings were smashed, and here and there a corpse littered the ground, releasing little plumes of blood swirling into the waters. Even the phosphorescent fish schools were gone, but Gray-Patch knew the way well and hurried as fast as she could in the murky gray dimness.

At her home she rushed inside to her apartment, but no one was there. She mind-tapped furiously everywhere but no response from children or neighbors, nor any sign of what had happened. Only emptiness. In despair she sank to her beautifully tiled floor. Where only hours before she had delighted in the luxurious surroundings of her fashionable city address, now she cared not in the least. Without her mate or children she was bereft. She slept fitfully until the dawn.

In the morning the city slowly came back to life. The pentapi had apparently left with their booty of slaves and treasure, and the citizens left behind emerged from their hiding places to see what remained of their homes and businesses. Orphaned children and desperate parents swam the streets searching for one another. This actually gave Gray-Patch a little hope. Maybe if she hunted long enough she would find her one little ones.

For hours she roamed along the avenues and side streets. Sometimes she passed happy reunions, and would pause for a brief moment to vicariously share in their joy. But mostly she encountered anxious searchers like herself, or sometimes the anguished flashes of those who had discovered those dear to them were gone forever. Even for those grieving souls she felt a twinge of jealousy, for at least they knew for sure what had become of their beloved, while she existed in a state of suspended emotions.

Day grew into night, and she realized she had not even stopped to eat. Reluctantly, she returned to her apartment, knowing a search at night would be useless. But then, as she took a shortcut down an alley near her street, she heard the faintest of mind-taps. She halted, not even sure it was real, but now it came again, a little louder.

"Mama?"

She whirled, sending out her own mind-tap. "Quicktail? Redtip? Where are you?"

"Here, Mother, here!"

And now she spotted them, emerging from the rubble of a collapsed villa, even now tentative and glancing in every direction but rushing to her as soon as they saw no danger was about.

"My children! My children!" Gray-Patch wanted to tell them how worried she had been, how much she had missed them, how she would never let them be separated again, but in the flood of her own emotions and the ones the children mind-flashed her she was overcome. For long minutes all she could do was hold them, and they too clung to her wings as if they were mere infants.

They set off the next morning. With her mate and brother dead, there was nothing left for Gray-Patch in the Great City. In the reefs surrounding the city the schools of fish and other reef dwellers flitted and swam about as usual, but only a few harvesters were back at work. Whether the rest were still in hiding, or had been captured or killed, Gray-Patch could not say.

They reached the ridge beyond which stretched the Barrens. Gray-Patch began searching for a suitable cave to stay in. An old ray swam slowly over, his fins stiff from age.

"Can I help ye find a place?" he asked her.

"Why you're the same ray who was here before!" she said. He had been old then, he must be truly ancient now.

"Oh, ye remember, do ye?" he said. "Well, I remember yeself too. Ye were nought but a niblin then, but now ye be full-grown, with niblins of ye own!"

Gray-Patch could not help smiling. "Yes, and we need a place for the night. Is there one available?"

"Oh, there be one or two, I think," he said. "Though we be nearly full-up. Seem many a ray hain't got the gumption for the Great City nowadays, and come by here for a spell. Whether they intend to stay or return, or something else entire, I can't say."

He showed them to a cave and languidly swam off to greet another visitor who had arrived. As soon as he was gone, her pups peppered her with questions.

"Who was that, mama?" "How did you know him?" "How old do you think he is?" "Do you think he ever met Slashtail the Warrior?"

"My children, slow down! I do not know how old he is, but I think Slashtail lived even before he did. He is simply a kindly one who helps travelers at this waypoint. And I met him years ago when I first came to the Great City from my home in the Southern Lagoons."

Her daughter, Redtip, nuzzled next to her. "Tell us about the lagoons, again, Mama."

"Well, it is warm there all the time, without the cold currents the Great City sometimes picks up. And there are not nearly so many rays as in the Great City, so that everybody who lives there is a cousin to all the others. The lagoon where your Uncle Surestroke and I grew up had the finest sand, so soft. Papa used to bring home the sweetest, biggest clams for us to eat."

"Will we see your mama and papa?" Quicktail asked.

"I don't know," Gray-Patch said. "Let's go to sleep. We have quite a journey ahead of us tomorrow." She stroked her pups and thought about her parents, wondering if they would welcome her back, or if they were even still alive.

The next day they crossed the Barrens in a reversal of Gray-Patch's own trip years before. She warned her children not to take in even a grain of the sand here, neither through mouth nor gill, not to stop along the way. Her pups were smaller than she had been when she had come this way, and not strong enough cross the Barrens without rest. Yet stopping here meant death, so she carried Quicktail and Redtip on her wings when they tired.

They did not come to the Sea Forest until the afternoon. This worried Gray-Patch, for they would not reach the lagoons until after nightfall, and it would be easy to become lost among the roots of the giant kelp in the dark. She also remembered the stories from her childhood of the dangerous creatures that lurked there, though she was not sure if the stories were true or merely meant to scare a young pup.

She decided the best course of action would be to stay just inside the edge of the Sea Forest, but within easy distance of the Barrens in case it was necessary to flee. She settled her children under her wings and found a shelter of sorts in the tangles of a huge plant. There would be no sleep for her this night, but she was happy to see Quicktail and Redtip fell asleep almost immediately. *They must be exhausted from the day's long swim.*

Well past midnight, she sensed motion in the water nearby. She could see a faintly phosphorescent outline, long and thin, like a reed passing by. She stiffened. Maybe whatever it was would simply continue by.

No, in a few moments she felt another movement, this time closer. She twisted her body and saw approaching through the roots and leaves that thing she had most feared: a giant eel. It was obviously aware of her presence, probably assuming her children to be an easy meal. It might be right, as at night it was in its element, and Gray-Patch at a disadvantage. Its grinning face neared, sharp teeth glinting. She knew she had only one chance to deter a large, aggressive predator like this. Its mouth gaped as it came and just before it snapped at her she struck with maximum speed and force, driving her tail's poisonous barb directly into its gills.

Her timing was perfect and her aim precise; the eel swam jaggedly downward, undulating and writhing in agony. If her venom did not kill him, it would certainly disable him for hours or days. It was only as she returned to the spot where her children slept that she realized the eel had hurt her, too. A shallow bite and a long perforation along one wing spilled blood into the water. In her intensity she had not even noticed her own wound.

The situation was urgent now, indeed. She did not think the wound too terrible, but the blood would attract all sorts of interest from predators.

"Wake now, my children!" she mind-flashed. "Quicktail! Redtip! No time to waste, we much be on our way!"

"In the middle of the night?" Redtip's mind-flash was drowsy and faint.

"Yes, right this moment. Follow me children and listen to my instructions carefully. You are to stay under my wings at all times so we do not become separated. If something happens to me, you two are to stay together."

"What could happen to you?" Quicktail asked. "Is there a giant squid? I can fight anything!"

"Don't you dare!" Gray-Patch said. "You are not full-grown yet, my pup. Promise me you'll do exactly as I say."

"Yes, mama," came the sheepish response.

"Now, if you two become separated from each other, you are to hide until daylight, and then swim as fast as you can to the south. Even if you get tired, don't stop swimming until you reach the lagoons. Do you understand me?"

"Yes, mama," her pups said.

As they traveled, Gray-Patch realized the wound must be deeper than she had first assumed. The intense but localized pain around the bite and cut in her right wing gradually spread until each stroke brought a wave of fresh pain. But at least it kept her awake.

The going was slow in the dark and murk, with Gray-Patch and her pups doing little more than feeling their way through the great root systems of the kelp. Every moment she was afraid of what they might meet.

But the night passed and gradually the faint light of early morning suffused the water. They could advance a little faster now, though Gray-Patch's wing prevented them from moving too rapidly. Still, she could see that the wound had knitted so she need not worry about leaving a blood trail.

By midday the roots thinned out and in the early afternoon they came to the canyon at the edge of the Southern Lagoons. It struck her when she had left she had been still a pup on the verge of adulthood. Now, she was a mature ray with pups of her own. She had seen things most rays never see, or at least don't live to tell about it.

"Quiet now," she warned Quicktail and Redtip. "Let me do the flashing when we meet someone."

They crossed the canyon and headed to her family's old lagoon. She still remembered perfectly well where it lay, although it surprised her how small everything felt. It had all seemed so big when she was younger! A group of elderly rays drifted lazily in the sunshine around the great pool from which the channels to the smaller lagoons veined out.

Before she could mind-flash the group to ask if they knew of her parents, two old rays were upon her, stroking her and inspecting her.

"Gray-Patch, is that you?" they asked. "Where have you been all this time? Why did you leave us? Do you bring word of your brother?"

It was her own mother and father, and she knew she was home. She was full of terrible news, but there would be time enough for that later. For now, she had brought the joyful gift of her children safely across a long distance and proudly presented her healthy son and daughter to their grandparents.

I'd like to thank all the people who helped me in the writing and production of this book. Since I wrote these stories over a period of years, I will undoubtedly overlook some of those who helped me. But I'm sure that Shea Megale, Steve Moriarty, Anita Klein, Angela Glascock, and many other members of the Writers of Chantilly, were chief among those whose comments and suggestions have done so much to improve this book.

I hope you enjoyed reading *A Far Ocean's Tale and Other Stories!* Because Amazon reviews are one of the main drivers of book sales for indie authors, please consider leaving a brief but honest review on this book's Amazon page.

Sign up for my mailing list and receive ***Orphan Stone***, the free prequel to the Last Days of Atlantis trilogy!

https://www.subscribepage.com/s8d7d6

Look for

O Trolly Night,

the first installation in the new

Hard Santa Case Files series,

coming in November 2023!

Made in the USA
Middletown, DE
16 September 2023

38539762R00106